MARY ANNE AND THE
SECRET IN THE ATTIC

My mind was reeling. This was almost too much to take in. I picked up one more letter, hoping it would help me understand more about this time I didn't remember.

"Dear Richard," it began. "We are glad to hear that you agree with our plan. Mary Anne is happy with us, and she is safe and secure here on the farm. Thank you for giving us this angel."

Oh, my lord. I couldn't believe what I was reading. My father had *given me away*. I threw down the letter and stood up. My legs felt shaky, and my head was throbbing. I'd wanted so badly to know more about who I was and where I'd come from. But now that I knew the awful truth, I realized I'd been better off before. I wish I had never found that letter. I left the attic without a second glance at the boxes that lay open behind me . . .

Whilst rooting around in her attic, Mary Anne comes across a secret she never knew . . . one she wishes she'd never discovered!

Una Miller JY5

MARY ANNE AND THE SECRET IN THE ATTIC

Ann M. Martin

Hippo

Scholastic Children's Books,
Scholastic Publications Ltd,
7-9 Pratt Street, London NW1 0AE, UK

Scholastic Inc.,
555 Broadway, New York, NY 10012-3999, USA

Scholastic Canada Ltd,
123 Newkirk Road, Richmond Hill,
Ontario, Canada L4C 3G5

Ashton Scholastic Pty Ltd,
P O Box 579, Gosford, New South Wales,
Australia

Ashton Scholastic Ltd,
Private Bag 92801, Penrose, Auckland,
New Zealand

First published in the US by Scholastic Inc., 1992
First published in the UK by Scholastic Publications Ltd, 1994

Text copyright © Ann M. Martin, 1992
THE BABY-SITTERS CLUB is a registered trademark of Scholastic Inc.

ISBN 0 590 55610 X

Typeset in Plantin by Contour Typesetters, Southall, London
Printed by Cox & Wyman Ltd, Reading, Berks.

10 9 8 7 6 5 4 3 2 1

The author gratefully acknowledges
Ellen Miles
for her help in
preparing this manuscript.

1st CHAPTER

"Mama! Mama!" Where was she? I felt so alone, even though a kitten was cradled in my arms, and even though some people were near me. The people (two of them) were very old. They weren't exactly strangers, but I didn't feel connected to them in any way. They stood and watched wordlessly as I called for my mother. "Mama! Mama!"

I woke up with a start, and it took me a second to realize that I was safe in my own room. The dream had been so real. I could almost smell the musty, closed-in odour of the big building I'd been standing in. I could almost feel the softness of the kitten I'd held. And I could almost understand the loneliness and the fear of the little girl who felt so all alone.

I rubbed my eyes hard, as if I could rub out the dream and the strange feelings that

1

went with it. I hated that feeling of lone-liness, and I hated not knowing where I was, and why those old people were staring at me. Actually, I wasn't even sure if the person in the dream *was* me—if she was, she was a very, very young me. One who knew how to say just one word. Mama.

By this time you're probably wondering who "me" is. I don't blame you. I am Mary Anne Spier, and I'm not *normally* a person who has weird dreams. I'm basically just your average, typical thirteen-year-old eighth-grader. I've lived all my life in a town called Stoneybrook, Connecticut. I have lots of good friends (including a steady boyfriend), a kitten named Tigger (he's grey, not black and white like the one in the dream), and a stepsister (who also happens to be one of my best friends) called Dawn Schafer.

What I *don't* have is a mother. I haven't had one since I was a baby. In fact, I really have no memories of my mother at all. I don't remember her being ill, and I don't remember her dying. So I suppose I can't say I miss her, since I didn't really *know* her. But I really miss having a mother.

My father has tried to make up for my not having a mother. He truly has done his best. But a father is not the same as a mother, no matter how hard he tries. My father used to be extremely strict with me, but over time he's begun to loosen up. I think *I* had to help him learn how to be a father to a teenage girl. There was a lot he didn't know, until recently. For example, my father didn't know that a seventh-grade girl should *not* be forced to wear her hair in pigtails and dress in childish pinafore dresses. My father didn't know that a seventh-grade girl is quite old enough to decorate her own room. I won't even get into all the other things my father didn't know about teenage girls, but I'm sure you can imagine.

I have always been very shy. I think this is because I grew up as an only child and got used to spending a lot of time alone. But in the past year or so, I have learned that being shy does not have to mean being timid. I have learned to stand up to my father and to challenge some of the rules he had made— just the ones that were obviously ridiculous, that is.

And I think my father learned to respect me as a person in my own right, instead of thinking of me as a helpless child. He learned that I am a responsible young adult who does not need someone hovering over her at all times. I also think that learning these lessons allowed him to feel free to get on with his own life. Which is how I got my stepsister!

Is that confusing? Okay, I'll try and explain. You see, I have a good friend called Dawn Schafer. I met her when she moved to Stoneybrook and became part of this club

3

I belong to, the Babysitters Club. (More about the club later.) Dawn moved here from California. She has long blonde hair and blue eyes. She has this laid-back attitude, mellow, but individualistic. And she loves health food like (ugh!) tofu burgers and (ugh!) soya milkshakes.

Anyway, as I said, Dawn moved to Stoneybrook from California, along with her mother and her younger brother Jeff. They'd left California because Dawn's mum had just got a divorce from her dad. And they'd come to Stoneybrook because that was where Mrs Schafer had grown up. So for Dawn's mum, it was like coming home to a place where she felt comfortable. For Dawn, it wasn't so easy. Connecticut is obviously pretty different from California. Dawn *hated* our cold winters, for example. But she adjusted quickly, partly because she'd joined our club and almost automatically gained a group of very good friends. The person who couldn't adjust was Jeff, her brother. In fact, he was so miserable here that the family decided he'd be happier going back to California to live with his father.

Anyway, I'm off the subject. What I meant to tell you about was the Great Romance. Here's the Great Romance, Part One: Dawn and I found out, while we were going through our parents' old yearbooks, that her mother and my father had gone out together when they both went to Stoney-brook High School. And here's the Great Romance, Part Two: After we "reintroduced" them, Dawn's mum (who I now call Sharon) and my dad (who Dawn now calls Richard) fell in love all over again. In fact, as you've probably guessed, they got married.

And are we now living happily ever after? Well, basically, the answer is yes. My dad and Tigger and I moved in with Dawn and her mum, and it took a while for us to get used to each other. The house is a really, *really* old farmhouse (it even has a secret passage that may be—*oooh!*—haunted). At first Dawn and I tried to share a room, but we soon discovered that we each needed our own space.

But we do get along pretty well, considering how different we are. My dad and I are both neat freaks (at least, that's what Dawn calls us). Did you ever hear the expression "a place for everything, and everything in its place"? Well, that's how my dad and I had always lived. We were organized, and tidy, and shipshape. Then we moved in with Sharon and Dawn.

Sharon is a wonderful person, and I love her very much, but she is most definitely not what I'd call a neat freak. In fact, she's the opposite. I'll give you some examples. One: Before she moved in with us, Sharon had never owned a vacuum cleaner. "Isn't a broom good enough?" she'd asked. Two:

Once I found my best shoes (which I'd been looking everywhere for) in the airing cupboard, under the clean towels. I've also found a box of cereal on the hall table, my *Sassy* magazine in the freezer, and a bottle of shampoo in my shoe bag. Three: After Sharon has cooked dinner (her meals often involve things like brown rice and seaweed), the kitchen could be officially declared a disaster area.

Of course, Sharon and Dawn have had to adjust to me and my father, too. And to Tigger. I know Sharon is not crazy about cats, but she tries hard to treat Tigger as a member of the family. And, I have to say it, a "family" is what we really feel like, and that feels great. I'll never call Sharon "Mum"—that name is reserved for someone I lost a long, long time ago—but she is about the best *stepmum* I could have hoped for.

You know, I'm not even sure what having a real mother would be like. Would I be less shy, less insecure if I'd grown up with my mother around? I suppose I'll never know. And I've got used to not knowing things. For example, I don't really know much about what my mother was like, or even how she died. I used to try to ask my father questions about those things, but I stopped. Why? Because I could see how much it hurt him to talk—or even think—about my mother. There's one thing I do know: He must have loved her very, very much.

Maybe this explains why, even though my life is very full now, with Sharon and Dawn and Tigger and Dad and Logan (he's my boyfriend), sometimes I still feel this empty place inside. And that's what I was feeling that morning, when I woke up from my strange dream. I felt that emptiness, and I felt alone, and I could completely understand the little girl in my dream. The one who was calling for her mama.

The *really* odd thing was that, as I woke up little by little, I remembered that I had had almost exactly the same dream not once but twice before. And all within about three weeks. I think this was what they call a recurring dream. I was starting to feel almost as if that big, musty building were a real place, and as if those strange people were real people.

I squeezed my eyes shut and then opened them wide. Even though it was already light outside, I didn't feel ready to wake up. I was still sleepy, but I was also afraid to go back to sleep. The dream had been very unsettling, and I didn't really want to repeat it one more time. Then I turned to look at my clock, and when I saw what time it was, I woke up *fast*. I was going to have to move it if I didn't want to be late for school!

I got dressed in a hurry, which wasn't too hard. I had laid out my clothes the night before, as I always do. That day I was wearing a pink sweater and jeans, with these cute little boots I'd just bought. I suppose you could say that my style is basically pretty preppy.

Then I headed for Dawn's room, to make sure she was up. "Morning," I said, knocking on her door. "Are you awake?"

She opened the door. "Yup," she replied, rubbing her eyes. "Come on in and help me decide what to wear."

Dawn's room was a bit of a mess that day. Clothes were flung all over the place. Her jewellery was scattered over her dressing table, and I counted about seven different shoes littering the floor. "How can you even have any idea of what clean clothes you have?" I asked, shaking my head.

"Oh, I know just where everything is," said Dawn. "For example, I'm thinking of wearing my denim skirt today, and it's hanging on the wardrobe doorknob. And with it, I'll wear my turquoise necklace, which is behind that book." She pointed to her bedside table. I picked up the book and saw the necklace. "See?" she asked. "Just as I told you."

I shrugged. "As long as the system works for you," I said. I've learned to live and let live. "Anyway, it sounds like you already know what you're going to wear. So let me tell you about this dream I had, while you get dressed." Dawn and I often tell each other our dreams. It's one of the things I

8

absolutely love about having a stepsister.

"Wow," she said, after I'd told her what I remembered. "Strange. So what do you think it means?" Dawn loves to analyze dreams, and usually she's pretty good at it.

"I have no idea," I said. "But it gives me the creeps. I feel like I need to puzzle it out."

We talked about the dream while Dawn got dressed and brushed her hair. And, since Sharon and my dad had already finished breakfast by the time we came downstairs, we kept talking about it as we ate our cereal. (I had Sugar Snaps. Dawn had Bran Flakes.) But no matter how hard we tried to analyze the dream, we didn't come up with anything that felt right to me. It seemed that the dream was going to be haunting me for a while longer.

2nd CHAPTER

"Hey, Mary Anne! Snap out of it!" Kristy snapped her fingers in front of my nose, and I blinked.

"What?" I said. "What's going on?" I'd been thinking about my dream again, and I suppose I'd kind of phased out for a minute.

"We're about to start the meeting, that's all," said Kristy, "and since you *are* a member, we'd like you to join us, if you think you can manage it."

Kristy was being sarcastic. She can be that way sometimes. It's funny—Kristy Thomas and I have been best friends ever since I can remember, but we are *such* different personality types. She's loud, and bossy, and sure of herself. And I'm exactly the opposite. But I suppose it's like the old saying, "opposites attract".

It was later that same day, and I'd been thinking about my dream pretty much nonstop since I had woken up that morning. All through school I'd thought about it, and all afternoon. By five-thirty, which was when our meeting started, you'd think I'd have been tired of thinking about it. But somehow it still had a grip on me.

I thought that maybe I could forget about my dream if I focused on something else, so I started to think about the BSC. What's the BSC? It's the Babysitters Club, of course. We call it a club, but it's really more like a business. Kristy thought it up. She's great at coming up with wonderful ideas. The idea for the BSC was the best one of all, and it's really one of the simplest. It works like this: Kristy and I and five other babysitters meet every Monday, Wednesday, and Friday afternoon from five-thirty until six. Parents phone us during those hours if they need to arrange for a sitter, and we work out which of us should take which jobs. We get plenty of work, the parents get a reliable babysitting service, and the kids get sitters who really love what they do. Everybody's happy.

The club has worked well from the beginning. We used to advertise with handouts and posters and things—and we still do, sometimes—but generally we have as much business as we want. The BSC has a great reputation in Stoneybrook.

Kristy's had some other great ideas for the club. For example, there's the club notebook. That's the diary that we each write in after every job we go on. Reading the notebook really keeps us up to date on what's happening with our clients. Another of her ideas was the Kid-Kits. We each have one: a decorated box, filled with colouring books and toys and stickers and all kinds of things that're irresistible to kids. It's not all *new* stuff. In fact, mine has my first Barbie ever, plus a battered game of Candy Land that I must have played three thousand times when I was little. But Kristy knew that even an old toy can look new and exciting to a kid. My Kid-Kit has been a real lifesaver more than once. It's just the thing for a rainy, dismal day.

Anyway, as you can see, Kristy is always having creative ideas, and she's really good at putting them into action. She's a real "do-er", as my dad would say. Nothing seems to bother her, either. Maybe that's because she's used to being in the middle of a lot of activity. Kristy comes from a large, complicated, chaotic family. Here's who she lives with: her mum, her stepfather Watson Brewer, her two older brothers Charlie and Sam, her little brother David Michael, her adopted baby sister Emily Michelle (she's Vietnamese), and her grandmother Nannie. Then, every other weekend and during the holidays, Kristy's stepbrother and stepsister Karen and Andrew come to stay. There's a cat, a dog, and two goldfish too.

Whew! It's lucky Watson is a millionaire (really, he is) and owns a mansion. That family just wouldn't *fit* in any ordinary house. Kristy seems to love being part of such a big family. I suppose it helps that she's so outgoing and assertive.

How else can I describe Kristy? Well, she loves sports and is a bit of a tomboy, she adores kids, and she couldn't care less about clothes or make-up or any of that stuff. She's happiest dressed in a poloneck, jeans, and trainers. She's pretty short for her age (like me) and she has brown hair and brown eyes (also like me). And, last but not least, she's chairman of our club.

The vice-chairman of our club is Claudia Kishi. It was Claud's room that we were all sitting in that afternoon. In fact, we *always* meet in Claud's room. Why? Because she has her own phone, with a private line. That means that we don't have to tie up anyone else's line while we take BSC calls. As vice-chairman, Claud doesn't really have any other duties, besides supplying the phone and the meeting place. But she does supply one other *very* important thing for the club: junk food. Munchies, snacks, sweets— Claud's kind of addicted to junk food, and she loves to share it.

It's hard to believe that Claudia eats as much junk as she does. For one thing, she has the most beautiful complexion, and for another, her figure is terrific. I suppose

13

she's just one of those people who is naturally gorgeous, no matter what she eats. Claud has a very exotic look. She's Japanese-American, and has lovely brown almond-shaped eyes and long, long silky black hair. She is a really sophisticated dresser: for example, that day she was wearing a lacy white top over a solid white body, a black mini skirt with white polka dots on it, lacy white leggings, and red high-top trainers. Also some really outrageous black-and-white jewellery (earrings and bracelets and necklaces) that she'd made herself out of papier-mâché. Claud's an excellent artist. You should see the portrait she once painted of Tigger.

Compared to mine and Kristy's, Claud's family is really small and, well, normal. It's just her, her mum and dad, and her older sister Janine, who is a true genius. Claud's really bright, too, but she'll never do as well in school as Janine does. She just doesn't seem to care about getting good grades. Except in art.

Claud's best friend is Stacey McGill. She's the treasurer of our club, which means that she collects subs every Monday. (Ugh! We all *hate* to part with our money.) Also, she keeps track of how much money is in the treasury. We use the money to cover what Kristy calls "overheads". It helps to pay Claud's phone bill, for example, and we also use some of it to pay Kristy's brother to

14

drive her to meetings. (When her mum married Watson, Kristy moved across town to that mansion of his. She *used* to live right next door to my old house.) Stacey's a real maths whiz, so the job is a breeze for her.

Stacey doesn't exactly *look* like the stereotypical idea of a maths whiz, however. She doesn't have slicked-back hair, and she doesn't wear black-framed glasses or carry pens and a slide rule in her pocket. In fact, her hair is blonde and curly (she often gets it permed), and she's just as cool a dresser as Claud is. I think that's partly why they're such good friends: they share a certain sophistication the rest of us just don't have.

Actually, Stacey may even be more sophisticated than Claud. She can't help it: she grew up in New York City. She didn't move to Stoneybrook until the seventh grade. Stacey's been through some tough times in the past few years. For one thing, she found out she has diabetes. Her body can't process sugars correctly, so she has to be very, very careful about what she eats. Also, she has to give herself daily injections (ugh!) of this stuff called insulin. Stacey's learned how to take care of herself pretty well, and I'm always impressed at how matter-of-factly she deals with having a life-long disease.

Also, Stacey's parents recently got divorced. Her dad lives back in New York, and Stacey goes to visit him as often as she can. But most of the time it's just Stacey and her mum against the world. (I can relate to that, since it was just me and Dad for so long.)

Anyway, despite her troubles, Stacey's one of the most cheerful, fun-loving people I know. And she *loves* being around kids, which makes her a great babysitter.

Now that you've met the chairman, vice-chairman, and treasurer of our club, I bet you're wondering who the secretary is. Well, it's me. (Surprise!) I really like my job, maybe because I'm naturally neat and organized. What I do is keep the record book up to date. The record book is where we write down all kinds of information about our clients—not just their names and addresses and their kids' names, but their kids' favourite foods, favourite games, allergies, and so forth. I love keeping track of those things. I also keep track of the club members' schedules, which isn't as simple as you might think. There are Kristy's softball games (she coaches a team called Kristy's Krushers), Claudia's art lessons, and Stacey's trips to New York to take into account, for example. And I have to be aware of the schedules of our alternate members, Logan Bruno and Shannon Kilbourne. They don't come to meetings, but they can fill in if we need extra sitters. Shannon lives in Kristy's new neighbourhood, and I've already told you that Logan is my boyfriend.

I've never had a problem keeping up with the record book, but if I ever couldn't make it to a meeting, Dawn would take over my job. In fact, she could take over *anyone's* job—she's what we call our alternate officer. I think Dawn's just as happy not to have a major job; she loves the club, but she doesn't exactly crave power or responsibility.

Now Dawn, Stacey, Claudia, Kristy, and I are all thirteen and in the eighth grade. But two of our club members are eleven years old and in the sixth grade. Mallory Pike and Jessi Ramsey are our junior officers. "Junior" means that they can only sit after school or on weekend days—no evening jobs unless they're sitting for their own families. This is fine with them, and fine with us. They get plenty of work, and we are free to do evening jobs.

Jessi and Mal are best friends and, like me and Kristy, they're a case of opposites attracting. Mal comes from a *huge* family (eight kids!), has red, curly hair, and glasses and a brace and likes to do quiet things like read and write and draw. She'd like to illustrate children's books one day. Jessi comes from a normal sized family (three kids), has black hair, brown eyes, and beautiful chocolate-coloured skin, and likes to spend her time dancing. She's studying to be a ballerina.

The two of them *do* have a lot in common,

though. They both wish their parents would stop treating them like children (Mal would love to get contact lenses; Jessi would like to be able to wear miniskirts), they both love to read (especially horse stories), and they're both great babysitters.

In fact, that day in Claud's room, Mallory was telling us about babysitting for her brothers and sisters the day before. Her face was lit up with excitement. "Nicky and Vanessa are both really into their Heritage Day projects," she said. "I think a lot of our regular clients will be, too. They're making a big deal of it at the elementary school. Everybody's supposed to do some kind of historical research—about their family tree, or about Stoneybrook, or about how their family *came* to Stoneybrook, or whatever. They're supposed to come up with projects, sketches and things, and then there's going to be a big fair where they can show off what they've learned."

Heritage Day sounded like fun—something to look forward to. I left the day's meeting with something new to think about, but you know what? I still hadn't been able to forget about my dream.

3rd CHAPTER

"Look at this one, Mary Anne!" Charlotte held up an old, sepia-tinted photograph of a serious young woman.

"Wow," I said. "Look at those plaits piled up on her head. Imagine how long her hair must have been when it was down!"

It was a Friday evening, after a BSC meeting, and I was sitting for Charlotte Johanssen. She's one of our favourite kids to sit for; she's fun to be with, and intelligent, and hardly ever gets into mischief. That day she was already hard at work on her Heritage Day project. Charlotte's a great pupil—in fact, she skipped a grade so that even though she's barely eight years old, she's in the third grade.

Charlotte had told me that everyone in her class was working on their family trees. Each pupil was supposed to research his family history, and find out when and why his family had ended up in Stoneybrook. For some kids the job would be fairly easy; if they'd moved to Stoneybrook recently, they wouldn't have to do much research. But a lot of families have lived in this town for generations, and Charlotte's was one of them.

"I asked Dad if he knew why his grandparents moved here," said Charlotte, who was still holding the picture. "But he didn't know. It's going to be really fun trying to find out!" Charlotte loves a mystery, and she's a pretty good detective. She couldn't wait to get started. It's great to see a kid so excited about a school project.

"Is that your great-grandmother?" I asked, still looking at the photo.

"Yup," said Charlotte. "See, here on the back it says her name: 'Berit Marie Hjielholt Johanssen'. I suppose Hjielholt was her name before she got married to my great-grandfather."

"It's so funny to look at this young woman and hear you call her your great-grandmother," I said.

"I know," Charlotte replied. "Isn't it weird to think that these people who I'm related to lived their whole lives so, so long ago? This picture is from when she graduated from college in Denmark."

I looked at the picture again. Charlotte's great-grandmother had been very beautiful. There was something about her eyes—they were large, and dark, and very expressive. Even though she looked serious in the picture, you could see a little spark of good humour in her eyes. I held the picture up next to Charlotte's face to see if there was any resemblance. At first, I didn't see any. The woman in the picture had blonde hair, and Charlotte's is brown. They both have dark eyes, but Charlotte's didn't look very much like her great-grandmother's. Then I saw it. The dimple. "Charlotte!" I said. "You have a dimple in exactly the same place as your great-grandmother had one!"

Charlotte grabbed the picture. "Let's see!" she said. "You're right. Hers isn't showing a lot, because she isn't smiling. That's just how mine is. But you can tell it's there. Cool!"

I could see that Charlotte suddenly felt connected to the person in the picture, and I was happy for her. But I have to admit that I also felt a twinge of jealousy. Charlotte had that picture, and a whole box of other pictures, scrapbooks, letters, and other things—all about her family. I don't think my father and I have any of that stuff. At least, I've never seen it. I think he got rid of it after my mother died, because looking at those things was just too painful for him. (Good thing he kept his high school year-books, at least. Otherwise I might not have a new stepsister now!)

I was starting to feel kind of sorry for

myself, but I snapped out of it when Charlotte's dog, Carrot, ran into the room. Carrot is a little schnauzer, and he loves to be in the middle of things.

"Carrot, no!" said Charlotte, as he started to nose through the box on her lap. "Out of kitchen!"

I laughed. It always sounds so funny to hear the Johanssens tell their dog to get "out of kitchen"—especially when you're in the living room, or the garage, or even outside. It's an all-purpose command and that just means "get out of here". Dr Johanssen, Charlotte's mum, started to say it when she wanted the dog out of the kitchen while she made dinner. But now they all say it, anytime and anywhere, because it's the only command that Carrot ever really pays attention to. (Well, he does know how to "say his prayers", by putting his paws in your lap and laying his head on them.)

Carrot scampered off—heading *towards* the kitchen, which made me giggle—and Charlotte and I went back to looking through her box. She pulled out a scrapbook full of yellowed newspaper clippings and leafed through it for a minute. "This would be great for the fifth-graders," she said. "They're doing this project of making a pretend 'one-hundred-year-old newspaper'. It's going to have all the news from Stoneybrook, but from a hundred years ago. They're going to print it and

22

everything!" She put the book aside and picked up a bundle of letters. "I'll have to spend some time reading these," she said. "They're from my great-grandmother to *her* mother, who still lived in Denmark. And look! The return address is Stoneybrook. They were already living here by then."

I reached into the box and pulled out an old photo album. "Who are these people?" I asked, pointing to a picture on the first page. It was a big group photo with a bride and groom in the middle of it. The men wore carnations in their buttonholes, and the women wore their hair in fancy buns. Nobody was exactly smiling—I suppose people didn't say "cheese" in those days— but they looked happy, anyway.

"Let's see," said Charlotte. She took the picture out of its slot in the book and looked at the back. "Oh, those are some cousins of my great-grandmother's," she said. "The Ottes. They were German."

Charlotte had obviously learned a lot about her family already. I could see that she didn't really need my help with her project, but it was fun to work with her anyway. We went through the whole box, checking to see what she would have to work with as she put together her family tree.

"This is the most fun project of all," said Charlotte, as she sifted through the box. "I'd rather do this than work on a sketch, or do the Stoneybrook history project, or anything. It's much more exciting to find out about your own family."

I nodded. "Hey, look!" I said, pulling a small, leatherbound book from the box. "This looks like a diary."

Charlotte glanced up, excited. "Really?" she asked. "Let's see." She opened the little book carefully and looked at the first page. "This is awesome!" she said. "It's my great-grandmother's diary, and it starts with her voyage from Europe." She leafed through it for a few minutes. "Wow," she said, in a hushed voice. "Here's an entry about her seeing the Statue of Liberty for the first time, as the ship sailed into New York Harbour."

What a find! Charlotte was going to have one of the best projects in her class, I was sure of it. While she was looking at the diary, I had continued to go through the contents of the box. It was nearly empty by now, but I felt around in the corners and came up with a delicate locket. It was gold, with flowers engraved on it. The initials B.M.H. were etched in fancy script on the back. There were tiny diamond chips in a half circle near the bottom. At the top was a link that could attach the locket to a chain. I showed it to Charlotte.

"Oh, it's so pretty," she said. "Do you think it has a picture inside?" She looked it over, trying to work out how to unfasten it.

"I can't get it open," she said, handing it to me. "Can you try?"

I checked the locket over until I found a little slit in the side where I could fit my thumbnail. Carefully, I prised the locket open. I recognized the girl in the picture straight away. "It's your great-grandmother again," I told Charlotte. "But she's younger here." In fact, she was just a little girl. She wore a high-necked white dress and high, buttoned boots, and white ribbons in her curly blonde hair. And she looked very much like Charlotte.

I gave the locket to Charlotte, and she held it and gazed at the picture. "We could be twins," she breathed. "Except for our hair. Only she was alive a hundred years ago. Isn't that incredible?"

A chill ran down my spine. I felt as if history were coming to life.

"I'm going to ask my mum if we can find a chain to put this locket on," said Charlotte. "Maybe I can wear it for special occasions." Her eyes lit up. "Maybe I can even wear it to the picnic!"

"What picnic?" I asked.

"Our school is having a special old-fashioned picnic the day before Heritage Day," said Charlotte. "There'll be historical games, and food like they ate in olden times, and if you want to, you can dress up in antique clothes! It's for kids *and* their

25

parents. My dad can't go, but my mum promised to take me."

"Sounds great," I said. I tried to sound enthusiastic, but once again I was feeling those twinges of jealousy. I'd *never* gone on a picnic with my mother. I'd never done anything with her. I'd never had the chance to ask her about her parents, or *their* parents, or any of that stuff. I had no idea how my mum's family had ended up in Stoneybrook—and I'd probably never be able to find out, since my dad wouldn't talk about her.

Charlotte kept on talking, telling me more about the picnic and about the other Heritage Day activities. But I wasn't really paying attention. I was thinking about my own particular family history, and about how little of it I knew. I was suddenly realizing that, in a very basic way, I had no idea who I was.

4th
CHAPTER

"See you soon, Charlotte," I said as I left her house later that evening. I'd made supper for her (string beans and fish fingers) and got her into her pyjamas by the time her parents came home. We'd spent most of the evening working on her Heritage Day project, and my head was spinning with the names of all of her relatives. The family tree was partly complete, and Charlotte was about to start on the "personal history" part of her project. She was going to try to work out exactly when and why her great-grand-mother had come to Stoneybrook.

"'Bye, Mary Anne," said Charlotte. "Thanks for helping me." She hitched up her pyjama bottoms, yawned, and waved to me as I headed out of the door.

As I cycled home, I thought some more about the photographs and letters we'd been looking through. Charlotte had her whole family history practically at her fingertips. All I had was my *own* history— the ticket stub from the "Remember September" dance I'd gone to with Logan, a sand dollar from a trip to the seaside, my Mickey Mouse ears from the time I went to Disneyland, and a few pictures from a holiday the entire BSC had taken in New York City. As much as I loved those souvenirs, I needed more.

I thought again about asking my dad about the past. I knew he could give me answers to some of my questions. But then I thought of how he'd looked that morning at breakfast, talking and laughing with Sharon. He was so happy since he'd married her and had put the past behind him. How could I do anything that might jeopardize that happiness?

By the time I reached my house, I was really feeling down. I slammed the front door and walked through the living room. I went into the kitchen and started opening cupboards, as if I was looking for something to eat. But the tins and jars on the shelves were just a blur. I wasn't even very hungry. There were two notes on the table, one from Sharon and my dad saying they'd gone out to a late dinner, and one from Dawn saying she'd gone the cinema. It was fine with me that nobody was at home. I felt like being alone.

I took some crackers and a glass of ginger ale into the living room and flopped down on the sofa. I picked up a book Dawn had been reading and flipped through it. *Ghosts I Have Known*, it was called. Dawn loves anything to do with ghosts, but I can take them or leave them. I put the book down, picked up the remote control for the TV, and pressed the on button. I ran through all the channels, but I didn't see anything worth watching for more than ten seconds. I turned the TV off, and watched the screen fade to black.

Tigger had jumped up onto the sofa, and he was sniffing at my crackers. They didn't seem to interest him, which didn't surprise me. They didn't even interest me, since they were the healthy kind that Sharon buys. No salt, no sugar, no white flour . . . no taste. "Oh, Tigger," I said, picking him up and burying my nose in his fur, "how can I find out more about who I am?"

Tigger purred and dug his claws into my shoulder, but he didn't answer, of course. Maybe I needed to talk to someone who could talk back. I decided to phone Kristy. I picked up the phone that sits on the end table and dialled her number. She answered on the second ring.

"Hello?" she said. I could hear shrieking in the background, and a dog was barking loudly.

"Hi, it's me," I said. "What's going on over there?"

"Hi, me," she said. "I'm sitting for David Michael and Emily Michelle, and they've just discovered a way to make Shannon bark. David Michael blows in her ear, and it works every time."

Shannon is a puppy. She's a Bernese mountain dog, which means she's a *big* puppy who's going to be a big, big dog. She's the sweetest, most gentle puppy I've ever seen, which is a good thing. She gets quite a workout from those kids.

"How are you?" she asked. "Are you home from your job already?"

"I've been home for a while," I said. "And I'm fine. Except—Kristy, does your family save stuff like old pictures and letters?"

"Of course!" she said. "Why?"

"Oh, it's just that—" I heard a sudden explosion of barking.

"Shannon!" said Kristy. "Hush. I'm trying to talk on the phone. David Michael, don't blow on her for a while, okay?" The barking stopped. "What were you saying?" she asked.

"Oh, nothing," I said. "I was just wondering . . . where does your family keep all that stuff? Is it stored away, or can you look at it any time?"

"It's in the attic, I think," she said. "Or no, maybe it's—" the barking started up again. "David Michael Thomas!" said Kristy. "I thought I told you to stop that!"

"Sorry." I heard David Michael's little voice.

"Okay," said Kristy. "Why don't you and Emily Michelle go and colour in in the study? I'll be there in a minute." I heard her sigh. "Sorry, Mary Anne. It's just one of those nights, I suppose. Now, what were you talking about?"

"It's not important," I said. I could see that Kristy was too busy to be bothered. "I'll talk to you tomorrow, okay?"

"Okay," she said, too distracted to notice that I was upset. "Don't forget we're supposed to go to the arcade in the afternoon, okay? I'll call you in the morning."

"Okay," I said. "See you." I hung up and sank down on the sofa. Now what? I wondered if I should just get a head start on my homework for next week, but I knew I wouldn't be able to concentrate. I couldn't stop wondering about family pictures and letters and stuff. Didn't we have *any*? I had foggy memories of looking at old photos when I was younger, but I was sure I hadn't seen any recently. It was hard to believe that Dad would have destroyed them or something.

Then I thought of what Kristy had said about where her family kept that kind of stuff. "In the attic," she said. Maybe, just maybe, if we had some of those things, they'd be in *our* attic. I thought back to when Dad and I had moved in with Sharon and Dawn. We'd worked all day, carrying boxes out of our old house and into the van, then out of the van and into Dawn's house. I'd been in charge of the kitchen stuff and the things from my room, and Dad had taken care of a lot of the other things.

Suddenly, I remembered something. I remembered Sharon looking at a pile of boxes that were stacked on the living room floor. "Where do these go, Richard?" she'd asked my dad. He'd barely looked at them.

"I'll take care of those," he said. He didn't even open them to see what was inside. Instead, he took them upstairs to the attic.

At the time, I hadn't stopped to wonder about what might be in those boxes. But now, all of a sudden, I was *dying* to know. Maybe we *did* have some family pictures! Maybe I could learn something about myself if I found them.

I grabbed a torch from the kitchen drawer and charged up the stairs. When I reached the door that leads to the attic, I stopped short. I realized that I'd never *been* in the attic before. And the thing is, this house can be kind of spooky. It has narrow hallways and low ceilings (people were shorter two hundred years ago when this house was built), and creaky floors. Not to

32

mention the secret passage. When I first moved into Dawn's house, I would get scared every time I heard a squeak or a creak. Then my dad explained that a house this old is always making little noises, and soon I got used to them. But it was one thing to become familiar with the main part of the house, and another thing entirely to think about exploring the attic for the first time. All alone.

I only paused for a second, though. I was too excited about what might be in those boxes. I pushed the door open and was greeted by a musty, stale smell. And darkness. But I could make out a steep, narrow flight of stairs. I shone my torch around, looking for a light switch. Guess where it was? At the *top* of the stairs! I started to climb, shining the torch on each stair before I stepped on it. The torch's beam was weak, but I was glad to have it. Finally I got to the top and turned on the light.

"Oh, no!" I said out loud. I was *surrounded* by boxes. Big boxes, little boxes, battered boxes, and boxes that were coming apart at the seams. How was I ever going to find the boxes I was looking for? I pulled one of them off a pile. "Linen" it said on top, in Sharon's handwriting. I knew better than to believe *that*. Sharon's so disorganized. I peeped into the box, and sure enough, instead of sheets and towels, I found Dawn's old stuffed animals inside.

I skipped over the next five boxes I found, since they all had Sharon's handwriting on them. Then, behind an old broken table, I found a box with my dad's handwriting on it. "Miscellaneous," it said on top. I pulled it into the light and opened it up. Right on top, I saw an old photo album. "Ah-ha!" I said.

I sat down right there with the album on my lap and started to look through it. The first pictures were from my parents' wedding. The one I liked best was an informal shot of the two of them walking towards the camera. My mum looks really happy, and my dad has this little smile on his face—he looks like someone with a wonderful secret.

The pictures seemed familiar, and I realized I'd seen them before. I kept leafing through that book, and then picked up another. Baby pictures! There I was, sitting on my dad's lap, smiling and wearing a little bonnet. I've seen baby pictures of myself before, but I'd never seen these particular ones. I looked cute, but the pictures got pretty boring after I'd seen two or three.

Then I turned a page and saw some pictures that really confused me. In them, I was still really, really young. I was sitting on a porch I didn't recognize, with an older couple I also didn't recognize. I was sure it was me, since I could see the little "Mary

Anne" necklace that I always wore around my neck. But who were those people? And where was that porch? There were other pictures, too: me and the two people sitting at a table, me and the two people under a tree. My hair was longer in some of the pictures, and my clothing was sometimes wintery and sometimes summery. Whoever those people were, I'd spent quite a lot of time with them. I looked closer at their faces. I even shone the torch on the pictures, but I couldn't work out who they were.

"Mary Anne!"

Oh, my lord. My father was calling me from downstairs. He and Sharon had come home while I was still in the attic! I shoved the album back into the box, tiptoed down the attic stairs, and slipped into my room. My heart was pounding a mile a minute. "I'm in my room!" I yelled, as soon as I could catch my breath. "I went to bed early. See you in the morning, okay?"

I lay awake for a long time that night, thinking about the pictures I'd found. Instead of finding out more about myself, I'd uncovered another mystery. I felt more confused than ever about my past.

5th CHAPTER

Saturday

I swear, Mal, when your family gets into a project, they _really_ get into it. Heritage Day has taken over the Pike household, totally and completely.

Tell me about it! At least you don't have to live with them. If I have to hear one more recital of Vanessa's poem, or listen to Claire go through her songs again, I think I'll scream.

Oh, it's not that bad. I had a pretty good time with the triplets— even if it _was_ kind of a morbid day.

I suppose you're right. It's not that bad. At least they're learning something, and it's great they're so excited. Still, couldn't Margo rehearse her play somewhere _else_ for a while? I'm starting to memorize her lines, I've heard them so often.

Stacey and Mallory were babysitting for Mallory's seven younger brothers and sisters that Saturday. And, because of Heritage Day, the Pike household was even more of a zoo than it usually is. Every kid had a project to do; every kid thought *his* project was the best; every kid needed help with his project.

"It's on days like these that I'm really, really glad my parents insist on two sitters for my family," said Mallory to Stacey. "There is just no way I could handle this on my own."

Stacey rolled her eyes. "No way," she agreed.

Margo was standing nearby on a low bench, practising her lines for the sketch her class was putting on. She's only seven, so she was having a little trouble with some of the words she was supposed to memorize. "My name is Felicity Jane Smith," she said, "and I am one of the original settlers of Stoneybrook. My father fled to this country to escape religious pros—pres—pers—"

"Persecution," said Mallory.

"Thanks," replied Margo. "Persecution."

"I don't know why they put big words like that in a play for second-graders," Mallory said under her breath to Stacey.

Stacey shook her head. "Seems silly to me, too," she answered. "But Margo's having fun anyway, so I wouldn't worry about it."

"Speaking of having fun, have you heard Claire sing her songs?" asked Mallory. "I think she's in the recreation room, with Nicky. Come on, let's see."

Claire *was* in the recreation room. She was dressed in high heels, a feather boa, and her favourite red swimsuit. "Hi, Stacey!" she said. "I'm a pilgrim!"

"You're the cutest pilgrim I've ever seen," said Stacey. "Let's hear the songs your class is going to sing for Heritage Day." Claire's at nursery school, and she just *loves* school.

Claire didn't need any prodding. She started right in with her song: "Oh, Susanna, don't you cry for me," she sang, "for I come from Anadama with a Band-Aid on my knee."

Stacey stifled a laugh. "That's great, Claire," she said. "What other songs are you singing?"

"Lots!" said Claire. "But I can't remember them all, so I'm just practising this one for now."

"How about practising somewhere else?" a voice said from the corner of the room. "I'm trying to get some *work* done here."

It was Nicky. He's eight years old and likes to boss his little sisters around.

"What are you working on, Nicky?" asked Stacey.

Nicky mumbled an answer.

"He's working on a family tree," said Mal. "Dad gave him all these old family papers and newspaper clippings and stuff, and he's trying to put the tree together. It isn't easy, since the Pikes have always had big families. Our great-grandfather had ten brothers and sisters!"

"Yeah," said Nicky. "And they all had names that started with 'P'. Pete Pike and Polly Pike and Prudence Pike and Paul Pike. I don't know how they thought *up* all those 'P' names."

"What about Patience and Patricia and Patrick and Percival?" asked Vanessa, who had come into the room behind Stacey and Mallory. "I can think of plenty of 'P' names."

"What's your project going to be, Vanessa?" asked Stacey.

Vanessa stood up straight and looked proud. "My class is going to recite a poem about the history of Stoneybrook," she said. "And I'm *writing* it!"

"Wow!" said Stacey. Vanessa's only nine, but she's wanted to be a poet for several years now. She can go for days at a time speaking only in rhyme. Stacey knew that if anyone could write a poem about a town, it was Vanessa.

"Want to hear the beginning?" asked Vanessa. She didn't wait for an answer. Plunging right in, she began, "In seventeen-hundred-and-ninety-one, Stoneybrook had just begun. The town was tiny but the people were strong—their spirit is still going strong!"

"Very nice, Vanessa," said Mallory, trying to cut her off before she gathered steam and recited the whole poem. "We can't wait to hear your class perform it."

"Speak for yourself!" said Byron, who had come into the room with Adam and Jordan trailing behind him. "That poem's going to be about six weeks long!" Adam's ten. So is Byron. So is Jordan. They're triplets. They're also jokers, always ready with a smart remark. The three of them were wearing hats that day, with little cards stuck in the brims. The cards said, "Press."

"We're ace reporters for the *Stoneybrook Historical News*," explained Byron. "And we're on to some hot stories."

"Yeah," said Jordan. "Like, 'First Horseless Carriage Comes to Town', and 'Moving Pictures Debut'. We're writing this newspaper with all the news from Stoneybrook's past."

"Except we're stuck," said Adam. "We've done as much research as we can in the school library, but we need more stories. Can you two help us?"

"I bet you could find some great ideas at the public library," said Stacey. "I've found great stuff there before. And Claudia's mum could help you since she works there."

"All right!" said Adam. "Can we go today?"

Stacey and Mallory exchanged a look. "I could take them," said Stacey, "if you could stay here with the others."

"Deal," said Mallory.

As Stacey and the triplets left the house, they heard Claire working on another song: "I've been working on the railroad," she sang, "all the ding-dong day!" And Vanessa followed them out, spouting rhymes until Jordan told her to button it.

Stacey had cycled to the Pikes', so the triplets got their bikes out, too, and the four of them cycled to the library. The reference room was pretty empty, since it was a nice day, and Mrs Kishi had plenty of time to help them find what they were looking for.

"Here's the microfiche machine," she said. "You can look through old issues of the newspaper and check for important news." Adam got to work. "And over here are the town records, where the births and deaths are recorded." Jordan started leafing through one of the oversized books. "And over here," said Mrs Kishi, "are some books about the history of Stoneybrook." She pulled one off the shelf. "This one may interest you," she said to Byron. "It was put together by the historical society, and it tells all the Stoneybrook legends that have been passed down through the generations."

Byron's head was buried in the book before Mrs Kishi even finished speaking.

"Thanks," said Stacey. "That's a great help."

Stacey picked up one of the other Stoneybrook history books and started to browse through it. But before she'd got through the introduction, which was kind of wordy, she heard Byron give a yelp.

"Wow!" he said. "Listen to this. There was this man called James Hickman, who was the richest man in town. He had a mansion and everything." He read a little further. "He was supposed to be really mean, too—and stingy. He lived all alone in a big old mansion."

This was starting to sound familiar to Stacey. "What did you say his name was?" she asked.

"James Hickman," said Byron. "But everybody called him Old Hickory."

Old Hickory! Stacey felt a shiver run down her spine. The BSC once had a midnight adventure at Old Hickory's grave.

"His grave is supposed to be haunted!" said Byron. By this time, Adam and Jordan were reading over his shoulder. "He died in his mansion one day—some people say he died of meanness. He was so stingy he didn't want to spend money even after he was dead, so he had left instructions that he didn't want a big funeral or a headstone or

42

anything. He just wanted to be stuck in the ground."

"Yeah?" asked Jordan. "Then what?"

"Then this nephew of his inherited all his money, and he felt guilty because there was no marker on his uncle's grave. So he put up this gigantic headstone, and they say that the ghost of Old Hickory was furious, so it haunts the grave!"

"Wow!" said Adam and Jordan together. "Cool."

"The cemetery is nearby," said Byron. "Can we go and see it?"

"Okay," said Stacey. They hopped on their bikes again, and soon they were exploring the cemetery.

"This is great," said Adam.

Stacey raised her eyebrows. "Creepy is more like it," she said.

The triplets started to look closely at the tombstones. "People died a lot younger in the old days," said Adam. "Look at this guy. He was only nineteen, and his wife was seventeen."

"Ooh, listen to this," said Byron, reading an inscription. "'How many hopes lie buried here.' That's for a little girl who died when she was only three. There's a picture of a lamb on it."

"Here's another one," said Jordan. "'Not lost but gone before.' That's kind of poetic. Vanessa would like it."

Stacey began to feel unnerved. The

cemetery was beautiful and peaceful, but it felt strange to be walking over people's graves. Just seeing their names on the stones—Sarah, Otis, Philura, Emeline—made them seem so real to her. She hurried the triplets along to Old Hickory's grave, which they thought was "really awesome". Then she took them home.

When I read Stacey's entry in the club notebook, I got an idea. Maybe if I went there I could find my mother's grave (which my father had never taken me to), or the graves of *her* ancestors. I'd never been terribly interested in finding out more about my "personal history", but now I was awfully curious.

6th CHAPTER

It took me over a week to pluck up the courage to go to the cemetery. I wasn't scared, exactly. Or maybe I *was* scared, but I couldn't tell you what I was scared *of*. I guess it was just that the idea of opening up my past seemed kind of overwhelming. There were times during that week when I could convince myself I was better off not knowing anything about my past, but my curiosity won out in the end.

I headed for the cemetery on a Tuesday afternoon. I hadn't told anyone I was going, not even Dawn or Kristy. This was something I had to do alone. It was a bright, sunny day, and as I biked to the cemetery I felt optimistic and brave. "What's the big deal?" I said out loud. "It's just a cemetery."

But when I paused at the big wrought-iron gates at the entrance to the cemetery, my palms started to sweat. My heart began to beat fast, and my breath was coming in funny little gasps. I decided to walk my bike around, just to give myself time to calm down. As I walked, I looked through the fence at the cemetery. It didn't look so scary in the daytime.

I thought about the adventure the BSC had had there, one Hallowe'en. The cemetery had certainly looked different at midnight on the scariest night of the year! These girls from school had tried to scare me into thinking that a necklace I had been wearing was a bad-luck charm. They thought they were tricking us into a terrifying night at Old Hickory's grave, but *we* scared *them* out of their wits! Still, it had been a nerve-racking night. I don't think I've been back to the cemetery since then.

By the time I'd walked all the way around the cemetery to the front gates I was ready to go in. I took a deep breath and held it—and then let it out with a giggle. I was thinking about when Mallory had told us that she and her brothers and sisters believe you should always hold your breath when you're near a graveyard. It's so the spirits won't bother you or something. Well, there was no way I could hold my breath the whole time I was in the cemetery, so I decided to forget about that old super-stition.

I started to walk along the main path

through the cemetery. It was quite a pretty place, if you could forget about all the dead people. ("People are *dying* to get into cemeteries!" is one of Watson Brewer's favourite jokes.) Anyway, beautiful big trees were shading the walk, and flowers had been planted near many of the headstones. I had thought the cemetery would be still and quiet, but instead birds were singing happily. I heard the sound of a lawn mower, too, and music coming from somebody's house nearby.

I saw some impressive monuments, like the one that marked Old Hickory's grave, and older, worn stones that must have been standing for a hundred years or more. I bent closer to look at some of the older ones. The writing was faded and hard to read, but the inscriptions were interesting. "There is rest for the weary," said one. "Sweet is the memory of the dead," said another.

That one reminded me of why I was there. It was because I *had* no memories. I decided to start looking for my mother's grave, but I didn't know where to begin. Little roads and paths led all over the cemetery. How would I ever find the place where she was buried? I needed a map or something.

I started walking, checking the names on every stone I passed. At first I looked for Spiers, but then I realized I should be looking for my mother's maiden name, too.

I knew she was buried near some of her relatives, and their name certainly wasn't Spier. Before she married my father, my mother's name was Baker. Alma Baker— isn't that a pretty name?

Someone with that name would have been kind and gentle and patient. Alma. It was such a calm, sweet name. I thought about my mother as I walked up and down the rows of stones, and I started to feel a little choked up. Still, I checked each name. My head was starting to spin. There were common names, like Smith and Brown. There were simple ones, like Fox and Bell. There were unpronounceable ones like Andrzejewski and Guadagnino, and ones that I thought were kind of funny, like Looney and Stumpf. (I had to giggle at those, even though I knew it was a terrible thing to do.)

But I didn't see any Bakers. The path stretched on in front of me, leading to an apparently endless row of headstones. I was beginning to feel frustrated. "I should *know* where my mother is buried," I said out loud, angry with my father for never bringing me to the cemetery. Then I saw something that wiped my anger and frustration away.

It was a simple headstone with a picture of a crane etched on to it. There was a small bouquet of wildflowers on the grave, and the yellow and white blossoms almost hid the name on the stone. But I brushed them aside to make sure I had seen the name correctly. I had. Yamamoto. And underneath that, a nickname: Mimi. Mimi! I felt a wave of sadness, and suddenly I missed Mimi so, so much.

Mimi was Claudia's grandmother. She lived with them for years—ever since her husband died—and so I knew her all my life. She died not that long ago, and I miss her a lot. She was kind of like a grandmother to me, as well as to Claud. She was a special friend. Mimi was comforting, loving, and dependable. If you were upset, she could always make you feel better. And if you were happy, she shared your happiness.

I stood for a moment looking at Mimi's gravestone, and then I began to cry. Now, my friends call me sentimental and oversensitive, because I cry so easily. I cry during the Movie of the Week, even if it's not *supposed* to be sad, and I cry when I read certain scenes in my favourite books, even if I've read them a million times before. So, I admit that I cry pretty frequently. But this time I was crying from somewhere deep inside, and this time crying didn't feel as good as it usually does. This time it really hurt.

Why was I crying? Well, the tears weren't only about Mimi. They were also about my mother—but they were connected with Mimi. Let me see if I can explain. Remember I said I knew Mimi all my life?

Well, that means that Mimi knew *me* all my life, too, including the parts of my life that I don't remember because I was too young. She knew me when I was first born, which means that she also knew my mother. So did other people, of course, but the thing is, I could have asked Mimi all about her, and Mimi would have told me everything she remembered. Mimi would have listened to me when I told her how confused I was about where I came from, and she would have comforted me. But Mimi was gone.

I stood there crying for a long time, until I realized I had to keep working on this mystery that was driving me crazy. "'Bye, Mimi," I said. "I miss you so much." I wiped away my tears, took one last look at Mimi's headstone, and left the cemetery. I'd had enough of that place for one day.

By the time I reached my house I had decided something. I was going to go back up to that attic, and I was going to keep looking through those boxes until I understood more about who I really was.

As soon as I got home, I headed upstairs. I decided I had about an hour before the rest of my family came home, so I knew I had to work quickly. This time, I didn't have to use a torch. Weak sunshine was coming through a dusty window at one end of the attic, and I dragged the boxes over to an old armchair that sat in the light.

I looked quickly through the first box,

reviewing the pictures I'd seen the last time I was up there. There were my parents again, on their wedding day. And there I was, baby Mary Anne, with those two people I hadn't recognized by the light of the torch. The sunlight didn't help—I still didn't recognize them—so I went on looking through the box. The rest of its contents were pretty boring: old spelling tests and social studies reports ("Alaska, Land of Contrasts") that I'd brought home to show my father.

I opened another box, which was marked "correspondence" and picked up a bundle of letters that lay on top. They were addressed to my father. I turned one of them over, looking for the return address, and my heart gave a jump when I saw what it said. The address read "Baker, Box 127, Old County Road, Maynard, Iowa". Were these letters from my mother to my father? Maybe I shouldn't read them. Maybe they were too personal. But I couldn't turn away from them. I picked them up, slipped the top one off the pile, shook the letter out, and began to read.

"Dear Richard," it said.

"We, too, miss Alma with all our hearts." Hmmmm. So it wasn't from my mother. My mother was already dead when this was written. I read on. "But Mary Anne brings us such pleasure every moment of the day. She is truly Alma's daughter: her bright,

51

sunny disposition is a joy. And she is so clever! Not half a year old, and already she knows our faces. We owe you thanks for sending her to us."

The letter was signed, "Verna and Bill."

Verna and Bill? Who were they? Why had I been sent to them? I picked up another letter and began to read. "Mary Anne smiled at Bill today," it said. "He nearly keeled over with delight." I read another one. "Enclosed is a picture of Mary Anne with one of our goats. Bill says he's sure our granddaughter will be a farmer's wife one day."

Suddenly my face felt hot and flushed. Granddaughter? That was *me*. I was Verna and Bill's granddaughter. They were my grandparents. Verna was my mother's mother! I had lived with them when I was a baby, and I didn't remember a thing about it. Not only that, I hadn't ever *heard* of these people! But suddenly I was sure they were the two people in the pictures I'd seen.

My mind was reeling. This was almost too much to take in. I picked up one more letter, hoping it would help me understand more about this time I didn't remember.

"Dear Richard," it began. "We are glad to hear that you agree with our plan. Mary Anne is happy with us, and she is safe and secure here on the farm. Thank you for giving us this angel."

Oh, my lord. I couldn't believe what I

was reading. My father had *given me away*. I threw down the letter and stood up. My legs felt shaky, and my head was throbbing. I'd wanted so badly to know more about who I was and where I'd come from. But now that I knew the awful truth, I realized I'd been better off before. I wished I had never found that letter. I left the attic without a second glance at the boxes that lay open behind me.

7th
CHAPTER

I lay on my bed, staring at the ceiling. I wasn't crying or anything—I was just lying there. I think I was in a state of shock. What I'd read had made me feel as if my whole life had been turned upside down.

"Mary Anne!" I heard Sharon calling from downstairs. "Dinner's ready. Come and help Dawn lay the table."

I opened my mouth to answer, but no sound came out. The last thing I wanted to do was eat dinner, but I was on automatic pilot. I swung my legs off the bed, stood up, and walked downstairs, feeling like a robot. Dawn was straightening the blue-and-white placemats that we use for everyday, so I marched over to the cutlery drawer and started to count out forks.

"Mary Anne!" said Dawn. "What's up? I didn't even know you were home."

I smiled at her—but it wasn't a real smile.

54

I just made the corners of my mouth curve up, and I knew it probably looked fake. Dawn didn't notice. She was busy folding napkins.

"Stacey and I went to the arcade today, and I got the cutest jumpsuit," she said. "It's turquoise, with a wide black belt. Wait'll you see it."

I didn't say anything, and she kept on talking. "Stacey got the same one in pink. I think we're both going to wear them to school tomorrow. Or would that be stupid? As if we were trying to look like twins?"

This time I *had* to say something, since she'd asked me a question. "Uh, no. No, it sounds fine," I said.

"Mary Anne?" Dawn asked sharply, looking at me more closely. "Are you okay?"

I nodded, feeling as if I might burst out crying if I tried to talk.

"Sure?" she asked doubtfully.

I nodded again, and she shrugged. "Okay," she said. "If you say so."

Dinner was a bit of an ordeal. Luckily, everybody else seemed to be in a chatty mood, and for a while nobody noticed that I wasn't talking much.

"The man from Sears called," said Sharon. "Our new washing machine is in, and they can deliver it on Friday."

"Great," said Dad. Then they got into a long discussion about the old washing

55

machine and its hilarious habits. Even Dawn had stories to tell, although she'll do almost anything to avoid doing laundry. They were talking and laughing and having a great old time with each other.

I sat silently, looking at my dad. This was the man who had given me away, the man who hadn't wanted me. But how did I end up living with him instead of with Verna and Bill, back in Iowa? Maybe the "angel" had turned into such a terrible child that my grandparents had decided they didn't want me either. Maybe they'd forced my father to take me back.

Dad wiped his eyes (he'd been laughing so hard he was crying) and gave me a curious look. "What's the matter, Mary Anne? Are you heartbroken at the thought of saying goodbye to that old washing machine?" That broke them up again, but I didn't even smile. Dad stopped laughing and looked at me again. "Are you all right, sweetheart?" he asked.

It made me angry to hear him call me sweetheart. If I was his "sweetheart", why had he given me away? A wave of sadness washed over me, but I tried to hide it. I put on my fake smile again and nodded. "I'm fine," I said.

Dawn put her hand to her mouth and whispered to Sharon and my dad. Something about me and Logan maybe having a row.

They all nodded wisely.

"May I be excused?" I asked politely. I skipped dessert and went straight to my room, where I stayed for the rest of the evening, pretending to do homework. At one point I heard a soft knock on my door. "Yes?" I asked.

"It's me," said Dawn. "I just wanted to let you know that I'm here if you want to talk."

"Thanks," I said.

"Also," she went on, "Logan called a little while ago, but I told him you couldn't come to the phone. I thought that was the right thing to say."

"Fine," I said. Poor Logan. He must be wondering what was going on with me. I knew I should phone him back, but I just didn't have the energy to pretend that everything was okay. I hoped I could explain the next time I saw him.

"Well, good night," said Dawn. She was treating me as if I were an invalid or something. I knew she would feel better if I told her what was going on, but I just wasn't ready to talk to anybody about it yet.

"Good night, Dawn," I said. "And thanks."

I got into bed and tried to read for a while, but it was no use. I couldn't concentrate at all. Finally I turned out the light and snuggled under the covers, hoping that I'd fall asleep soon. Sleep would be a relief;

I could stop thinking about my awful discovery.

I tossed and turned for a long, long time, but I must have fallen asleep eventually, because the next thing I knew, I was waking up with a start. "Mama!" I was saying. I'd had that dream again. In it, I'd been sitting on an old porch swing, between two people. The kitten was on my lap again, and I'd been patting its soft fur. But even though the people were there and the kitten was with me, I felt very alone.

I lay there for a minute, thinking about the dream. Then, suddenly, I sat straight up in bed. I'd realized something. That dream didn't come out of nowhere! It came out of my memory. That little girl was me, and the people were Verna and Bill. And the reason I felt so lonely was because I missed my mother and father.

I felt a tear slip down my cheek. That little girl hadn't even been old enough to realize that her mother had died—and that her father didn't want her any more. All she knew was that they weren't there with her. It didn't matter that the people taking care of her were kind and gentle; they were strangers to her, and she felt lost.

I looked over at the clock. It was after two A.M., but I knew there was no way I was going to be able to go back to sleep now that I had discovered the truth about my dream. And knowing one truth only made me hungry for more. It was time to return to the attic.

I found my torch and stepped quietly out of my room. The house was silent; everybody else was peacefully asleep. I opened the attic door carefully, so it wouldn't squeak, and closed it behind me as I slowly climbed the stairs. The torch beam was weak: it barely lit the way through the total darkness of the narrow staircase. I reached the top and flipped on the light. There was a sudden scurrying in the far corner of the attic, and my heart began to pound. "Just a squirrel," I whispered to myself. "Nothing to be afraid of." I tiptoed over to the chair and the boxes I'd left open. My heart was still racing, and I could hardly breathe in the musty stillness of the attic.

I reached into the box and pulled out a handful of letters. Then I sat down in the big chair. I held the letters tightly in one hand, looking at them. I took a deep breath and opened one of the letters.

"Dear Richard," it said. "Mary Anne grows and changes every day. Bill and I feel so lucky to have her." It went on to describe all the things I'd done recently: I'd patted the goat, smiled at a neighbour, pulled the cat's tail (by accident!)—stuff like that. Then, at the end of the letter it said, "You can rest assured that you made the right decision when you sent Mary

Anne to us. She'll grow up healthy and strong here."

I closed my eyes tightly. It was so hard to believe that my father had given me up. Why had he done it?

I opened my eyes and read another letter. "Enclosed is a picture of Mary Anne on her first birthday," it said. "She is a delightful child." I felt another stab of pain. My father hadn't even been with me for my first birthday party! I suppose he just hadn't cared about me.

I sat for a minute in the dark, stuffy attic, gathering my thoughts. Every letter I had read so far had only made the hurt worse. Should I keep reading, or should I stop? I felt shaky from lack of sleep. But I still had questions that hadn't been answered. Why had I been sent to my grandparents? How long had I stayed there? And why had I been sent back to Stoneybrook? I decided to keep reading.

"Dear Richard," said the next letter I picked up. "We understand your desire to spend some time with Mary Anne."

I heaved a huge sigh of relief when I read that. He *had* wanted to see me! I read on.

"I'm afraid, though," it said, "that we feel it would be too disruptive at this point for her to travel halfway across the country. Enclosed are some recent pictures. Perhaps they will satisfy your need to see your daughter."

60

I picked up another letter and read it eagerly. I was dying to know what happened next. "Dear Richard," it said. "There is no need to be so vehement. Of course we believe that you are now ready to 'be a father' again. But are you really sure you are capable of taking care of a little girl as well as we can? After all, you are a man alone. A little girl needs more than just a father."

I held my breath as I picked up the next letter. Would my father insist on having me back? Would he fight for me? "Dear Richard," it said. "If you are sure you are ready to take care of your daughter, we are willing to let her come to you. But remember, you gave her to us. And we are not ready to let her out of our lives forever. We want you to show us she will be raised correctly. She is almost eighteen months old now, and we have given her what we could. We entrust her to your care for now. But remember, she is as much ours as yours."

I put down the letter—it was the last one in the bundle—and stared into the darkness of the attic. So my father *had* wanted me. Enough to insist on my return to Stoneybrook. But my grandparents had wanted me, too. Did they have a legal claim to me? Maybe this explained why my father had been so strict with me when I was younger: he had to prove he was a fit father. Otherwise, I could have been returned to my grandparents' custody.

I wondered if they were still alive. What if they were? What if they still had a claim to me, and what if they decided to act on it? Suddenly, my whole life felt up in the air. Who did I belong to?

I couldn't believe I'd never known about any of this until now. Why hadn't I been told? Why had my father kept it such a secret? And other people must have known, too: Mimi, Kristy's mum, Claud's parents. Maybe Kristy's older brothers even knew! I felt angry. Why was I the last one to know about my own self?

It was all too much to take in. I leaned back in the chair, too exhausted to walk down the stairs and go back to bed. I thought for a long time about what I'd learned. I must have dozed off. The next thing I felt was the rising sun on my face. I had spent the night sleeping in that attic.

8th CHAPTER

It wasn't easy getting through a day at school after sleeping in the attic. I was tired, for one thing, since I hadn't slept very long. Also, I had a terrible crick in my neck from sleeping in the chair. And, of course, I was still in shock about what I'd discovered reading those letters. All day, I felt incredibly strange and out of place. Nothing looked or felt familiar, and it took a lot of energy to remember where my classes were and how I was supposed to act with my friends. I wasn't thinking much about what I'd read in those letters; my mind was almost a blank. I didn't want to think about my past any more. I realized I'd been better off before, not knowing.

I skipped lunch so I wouldn't have to sit with my friends. I knew I wouldn't be able to laugh at any of Kristy's nauseating jokes about the cafeteria food, or pay attention to

Dawn when she talked about some cute boy in one of her classes. I also didn't want to face Logan, and explain why I hadn't come to the phone the night before. It was easier to hide out in the library, reading *Wuthering Heights* for the millionth time, nibbling at my sandwich.

When school ended, I told Dawn I wouldn't be walking home with her because I wanted to clean out my locker. She gave me a weird look, but luckily she didn't question me. I dawdled for as long as I could, and then walked home slowly, kicking a stone the whole way. When I got home, I went right to my room and stayed there, patting Tigger and staring out the window over my bed.

At five o'clock I heard a knock on my door. "Mary Anne," said Dawn. "It's almost time for our meeting. Want to walk over to Claud's with me?"

Oh, no. Of course, it was Wednesday. I'd forgotten that we had a BSC meeting. Now I was going to have to sit in Claud's room and pretend everything was normal. I knew there was no way I could get out of going; I'd been at school that day, so I couldn't pretend to be sick. But I did not want to walk to BSC headquarters with Dawn and have her question me about my weird behaviour.

"No, I'm finishing off my book report," I lied. "I'll cycle over as soon as I've finished."

"Okay, see you there," she said. I heard her run down the stairs. I almost called after her, to ask her to wait for me. I had a sudden impulse to tell her everything. Maybe I would be relieved to talk about it. But then I heard the front door slam, and the impulse passed. Better to keep it to myself for now, I thought. I didn't want to deal with other people feeling sorry for me—I was having enough trouble dealing with my own feelings.

I lay staring into space for another fifteen minutes, and then realized I'd better get going if I didn't want Kristy to be annoyed with me. She *hates* it when any of us members are late for a BSC meeting. I hopped onto my bike and pedalled over to Claud's, headed inside (none of us have to knock, we're expected), and sprinted up the stairs. I arrived in Claud's room a little out of breath, but just in time to hear Kristy say, "Order!"

Kristy was sitting in the director's chair, as she always does. She nodded at me as I took my usual seat on Claud's bed, between Dawn (who was wearing her new turquoise jumpsuit) and Claudia. Stacey (wearing the pink twin to Dawn's jumpsuit) was sitting in Claud's desk chair, drawing on her trainer with a fancy felt-tip pen. Jessi and Mal sat near her. Jessi was putting tiny plaits into Mal's hair. "This'll look

65

incredibly cool after you sleep with them in," she said. "Trust me."

"I trust *you*," said Mal. "I just don't trust my hair. I never know *what* it'll do."

"Ahem," said Kristy. I could tell she was about to make some official-sounding statement abut the meeting having begun, but just then the phone rang. Kristy, Stacey, and Claud all dived for it. I just sat there.

"Hello?" said Stacey. She'd grabbed the phone first. "Babysitters Club." She listened for a moment. "Of course, Mrs Rodowsky. We'll call you right back." She hung up. "Mrs Rodowsky needs a sitter for Friday afternoon and evening."

There was a silence. I realized everyone was looking at me, as though they expected something of me. I blanked out for a second.

"Mary Anne," said Kristy. "We're waiting."

Waiting? For what? I looked down at my hands, trying to gather my thoughts. Then I saw the record book, which was sitting on my lap. I felt really stupid. "Uh, just a second," I said, flipping it open. "That's Thursday the twelfth, right?"

"Not Thursday," said Kristy. "Friday. Mary Anne, what's the matter? Are you okay?" She looked at me closely.

"I'm fine," I said. "Just fine. Now, let's see. It looks as if Jessi and Dawn are the only ones available."

"But I can't do it," said Jessi. "It's not just for the afternoon, and I'm not allowed to sit at night."

"Oh, right," I said. "Okay, then, so Dawn has the job." I marked her name into the calendar, and Stacey called Mrs Rodowsky back.

I looked up and saw that Kristy was still looking at me. She seemed puzzled. "Mary Anne, you're off in outer space," she said. "What's up?"

It was just my luck that the one time Kristy decided to be extra-sensitive was the one time I didn't wish to talk about my problems. "I'm fine, really," I insisted. I gave her my best "corners-up" smile.

"I thought she'd had a row with Logan," said Dawn. "She's been like this since last night. But I talked to him today, and he said they were getting along just fine." She shook her head.

"Maybe she's upset about something that happened at school," suggested Jessi.

"No, she'd have told me," said Dawn.

I listened to them talk about me as if I weren't there. And you know what? It didn't really even bother me, because I *felt* as if I wasn't there. Pretty soon the phone rang, and they dropped the subject.

"Mrs Perkins!" said Claud, who had answered the phone. "How are the girls? I haven't seen them for ages." She listened

67

for a minute. "Myriah has a loose tooth," she told the rest of us, relaying the information, "and Gabbie and Laura have just got over chicken pox." She listened again. "Of course," she said. "I'll get back to you in a minute." She turned to me. "Mary Anne," she said, "Mrs Perkins is looking for somebody for Saturday—not Friday, but Saturday—afternoon." Her eyes twinkled. She was making fun of me, in a friendly sort of a way.

I checked the schedule, told her who was available, and pencilled in Mal's name once we'd decided that she should have the job. I was beginning to function a little better.

"I hear Myriah's class is doing a great project for Heritage Day," said Stacey. "They're going to make a mural about Old Stoneybrook, and it's going to be on display at the fair. Some of the fifth-graders are helping them."

"You know," said Kristy, "I've been thinking about Heritage Day. The reason for having it is to raise money for the Historical Society, right?"

"That's true," said Claud. "I'd sort of forgotten about that. Everybody's so caught up in their projects that the fund-raising has almost been forgotten. But my mum says the Historical Society really needs money for renovating that old sawmill."

"Well," said Kristy. "I think the BSC

should contribute somehow. Like have some kind of a stall."

"Great idea!" said Claud. "How about a face-painting stall? I love painting little kids' faces, and they look so cool walking around afterwards."

"Face-painting is fun," agreed Dawn. "But it doesn't have much to do with the history of Stoneybrook. We should do something historical."

"Like what?" said Mal. "I was thinking of a bakery stall. I suppose we could bake stuff from colonial recipes—"

"Too much research," said Jessi. "Let's keep it a little simpler."

"I know," said Stacey. "Last time I was in New York, I saw these people with big cardboard cut-out figures of people like the President and Bart Simpson. They'd take your photo with the figure, and it would come out looking as if you had posed with the real person. It was cool!"

"I love it!" said Claud. "I'm sure we could make our own cut-outs."

"It sounds like fun," said Kristy. "But Bart Simpson and the President don't have much to do with Stoneybrook. Who else could we make?"

"How about figures from the history of Stoneybrook?" said Mal. I nodded. That sounded like a great idea. Even I couldn't help feeling a little excited about a new BSC project. I wasn't ready to *participate* exactly, but at least I was paying attention.

"Like maybe Old Hickory?" said Jessi.

"Yeah!" said Kristy. "And maybe Sophie. Remember? The girl in that old painting we found in Stacey's attic?"

"How about George Washington?" said Claud. "And Martha, too. I don't know if he was ever in Stoneybrook, but there's a big sign in Greenvale saying 'George Washington slept here'—and Greenvale's only fifty kilometres away. That's close enough, isn't it?"

Stacey looked excited, but just as she was about to get into the discussion, the phone rang and she grabbed it. She talked for a minute before hanging up, while everybody else kept offering suggestions for our cutouts. "That was Dr Johanssen," she said. "She feels awful, but something came up and she can't take Charlotte to the parent-child picnic. Mr Johanssen can't go either. Charlotte was sort of hoping I could take her, but I can't. I already have a job that day. Who else is available?"

I checked the book, without having to be reminded this time. "I suppose I'm the only one," I said.

"You don't sound very enthusiastic," said Stacey. "Are you sure you're okay, Mary Anne? You've hardly said a single word the whole meeting."

"I'm fine," I replied, for what felt like the thousandth time. "And I'll be glad to take Charlotte to the picnic." I was even gladder that it was six o'clock by then. Our meeting was over, and I could go back to my room and stop having to pretend to be fine.

9th CHAPTER

As I cycled home from the meeting, I thought how strange it had been to be with my friends—and yet *not* to be with them. It was if I'd been *observing* my friends; as if I were some kind of anthropologist. Do you know what that is? We learned about anthropologists in my social studies class. They are scientists who study people's behaviour. Some of them visit tribes who live deep in the jungle, and observe the way they live their lives. The anthropologists document the way the tribes bring up their children, how they behave when they're in love or at war—that kind of stuff. Anyway, at the BSC meeting I'd felt like an anthropologist observing the ways of the typical American teenage babysitter.

You probably think I am pretty strange.

I was even beginning to think I was strange. I realized that it was time for me to rejoin the human race—as a member, not just as an observer. And I knew that the only way to do that was to tell someone what I'd been going through. Maybe if I shared it, got it out in the open, I could start to deal with it.

I decided to call Logan. I knew he must be wondering what was going on, since I hadn't talked to him in days. I hadn't been fair to him.

As soon as I got home, I headed for the study. Dawn had gone on to the Pikes' to help Mal sit for her brothers and sisters. Dad was making dinner in the kitchen, and Sharon was doing something upstairs. I didn't know how long I'd have the study to myself, so I picked up the phone right away and dialled Logan's number. I was feeling pretty nervous about talking to him, but as the phone rang at his house I kept telling myself that I was doing the right thing.

"Hello?"

Oh, no. Logan hadn't answered the phone. It was his mother, instead. "Hi, Mrs Bruno," I said. "This is Mary Anne. Is Logan there?"

"Hi, dear," she said. (Mrs Bruno has this great Southern accent, just like Logan's. The Brunos moved here from Louisville, Kentucky.) "No, I'm sorry, he's not. He's just out doing an errand for me, though. He should be back any minute."

73

"Could you ask him to phone me when he gets in?" I asked. "It's—it's pretty important."

"Okay," she said. "I'll pass on the message. I'm sure he'll be glad to hear it."

"Thanks," I said. After I'd hung up the phone, I rubbed my sweaty palms on my jeans. I hadn't been so nervous about talking to Logan since we first started to go out! I sat right there on the sofa, waiting for the phone to ring. Mrs Bruno *had* said that Logan would be back any minute. I picked up a magazine and flipped through it, but I couldn't concentrate.

I rehearsed what I would say to Logan when he phoned. "Logan, I'm sorry I've been so distant lately. It's just that I found out the most terrible thing. My own father gave me away when I was a little girl!" Logan would ask a million questions. He probably wouldn't believe me at first, and I'd have to tell him about the letters. Then he'd want to know why I hadn't *stayed* with my grandparents. "I don't know," I'd say. "I suppose my father decided he wanted me after all. But my grandparents wanted me, too—and maybe they still do. I might have to move to Maynard, Iowa!"

Logan would probably be just as upset as I was, but I was sure he'd find something soothing to say. And maybe he could help

74

me work out what to do next, now that I knew about the Big Secret of my past.

I sat there, biting my nails and waiting for the phone to ring. Where *was* Logan? His mother had said he'd be back any minute. I checked the clock. That had been seven minutes ago. Maybe he'd got into some kind of trouble on his way home. Maybe he was hurt. I shook my head. I knew I was getting carried away. Then I had another thought. What if he *was* already at home, and he wasn't phoning me because he was angry with me for not speaking to him lately? My stomach felt like it was tied in a big knot. Maybe I should phone him again, and apologize really quickly before he could hang up on me. I reached for the phone.

Just as I touched the receiver, the phone rang. I nearly jumped out of my seat. I grabbed the phone, thinking quickly what to say to Logan. But before I could say anything, I heard my father say, "Hello?" He must have picked up the extension in the kitchen. I was just about to say, "It's for me, Dad," when I heard a tiny, creaky voice at the other end. "Richard?" it said. "Is that you?"

That didn't sound like Logan. I should have hung up immediately—I know it isn't right to listen in on other people's conversations—but I was curious. Who belonged to that voice? It was one I'd certainly never heard before.

My father sounded as if he didn't recognize the voice, either. "This is Richard Spier," he said. "Who's calling, please?"

"Richard, this is Verna Baker."

My father didn't say anything for a second. I wondered if he was as shocked as I was to hear the name. I almost dropped the phone. I had to put my hand over the receiver so that neither of them could hear my breathing, which was suddenly kind of loud. Verna Baker! My grandmother.

"Verna," said my father finally. "Well. It's been a long time."

"Yes, it has," she answered. "A very long time. Mary Anne must be—how old now? Twelve?"

"She's thirteen," said my dad.

"Thirteen years old," mused my grandmother. "I can't imagine what she looks like."

Wow. That meant that Dad hadn't even sent them a photo for a long time. He probably hadn't had any contact with my grandparents for a while.

"More like her mother every day," said my father.

Another shock! He'd *never* told me that.

My grandmother sighed. "I'm phoning, Richard, with some sad news. Bill passed on last week—a coronary."

"I'm so sorry," said my father.

"I'm sorry, too," said my grandmother.

"I'm sorry he didn't get to see his granddaughter again before he passed away."

She sounded angry.

"My understanding was that the two of you decided it would be better that way," said my father. He was working hard to be patient.

"That was our original decision," said my grandmother. "But it wasn't an easy one—and I'm not sure any more that it was the right one."

"What do you mean?" asked my father.

That was exactly what *I* should have asked. What did she mean? Did she mean she was sorry she'd given me back?

"I mean that the loss of Mary Anne has been a heartache for both of us for all these years."

"I'm sorry," said my father again. He sounded sort of helpless.

"I want her to come here," said my grandmother.

What? I couldn't believe my ears. This was exactly what I'd been afraid of.

"What?" asked my father, echoing my thoughts.

"I want her to come to me," said my grandmother. "I don't want to die without seeing her. She is my only living flesh and blood now."

"Well, I don't know, Verna," said my father. "Mary Anne is a happy, well-adjusted girl. She doesn't remember anything about that time, and I'd rather keep it that way. Bringing up the past would only be painful for everyone."

"Richard, you haven't changed a bit," said my grandmother. "You're as stubborn as ever. You got your way all those years ago, and I want to get *my* way now. I can be just as stubborn as you. I want Mary Anne to come to Maynard."

"Verna," said my father. "I'm sorry about Bill. He was a good man, but I can't let you do this. Mary Anne stays here."

I was *so* happy to hear Dad say that.

"I won't take no for an answer, Richard," she said. "We're going to have to work this out, just like we did before."

At that point, I was too upset to listen any more. I hung up the phone gently, hoping neither of them would hear the click. Then I sat back on the sofa and let out a deep breath. If I'd felt confused and scared before, it was nothing compared to how I was feeling *now*. My whole life was in the balance. I'd lived in Stoneybrook ever since I could remember. All my friends were here, and all the family I knew—or cared to know. And now it looked as if I could spend the rest of my life in Maynard, Iowa, with an old lady who was a complete stranger to me. And she wasn't the *nicest* old lady, either. She didn't sound like a kindly cookie-baking grandmother. She sounded like a rock-hard negotiator who was going to go after what she wanted. And what she wanted was me.

I couldn't even cry.

"Mary Anne?" Dawn had come into the study. "I've just got back from the Pikes'. What's the *matter*?"

I must have looked awfully upset. And suddenly, I found that I *could* cry, after all. "Oh, Dawn," I wailed. "It's terrible. You won't believe it."

I told her everything, between sobs.

"Mary Anne," she said, looking worried. "Come on, stop crying. Please?" She hugged me. "It's going to be okay . . . I think."

"D-did you know about this?" I asked, wiping my eyes with the tissue she'd given me. "I bet everyone knew but me."

"No way," she said. "If Richard ever told my mum anything about it, she certainly didn't tell me. I'm as shocked as you are." She hugged me again. "Listen," she said. "You're my sister. There is *no way* I'm going to let you be shipped off to Maywood, Ohio."

"Maynard," I said miserably. "It's Maynard, Iowa." I had started crying again as soon as she called me her sister.

"Whatever," she said. "Don't cry. Let's calm down and talk this over. I'm sure we can work something out."

We talked for the rest of the evening, but by the time we went to bed (I was totally exhausted by about nine o'clock) we hadn't worked anything out. Telling Dawn had made me feel a little better, but it didn't exactly solve anything. The big question still stood: Did my grandmother have a legal claim to me?

10th CHAPTER

Friday

If some Hollywood producers ever got to know Jackie Rodowsky, they could make a million bucks with a film about that kid. Of course, they'd need to hire a stuntman (stuntboy?) to do the things that Jackie does in real life. But the Jackie Rodowsky Story would be full of thrills, chills, and suspense. Will Jackie survive another fall down the stairs? Will Jackie be able to put together the lamp he broke before his mum gets home? Will Jackie's baby sitter have a nervous breakdown? The tale of Jackie,

81

the Walking Disaster, will be coming soon to a cinema near you.

As you can probably guess from Dawn's notebook entry, sitting for the Rodowsky boys is always a challenge. They do know how to keep you on your toes—especially Jackie. We call him the Walking Disaster, because trouble always seems to find him, but it's a fond nickname. We really like Jackie a lot, and we like his brothers, too. It's just that you never quite know how the day will turn out when you first arrive at their door.

When Dawn turned up that Friday afternoon, Mrs Rodowsky was more than ready to leave. Dawn wasn't late; we make a point of being a little early for jobs. But Mrs Rodowsky looked as if she badly needed some time off from those three boys. She was all ready to escape the second Dawn arrived. "'Bye!" she said to the boys, waving over her shoulder as she dashed to the car. "Be good!"

Well, I'm sure Jackie and his brothers would *like* to be good. I'm sure they really try hard sometimes. But somehow "being good" is just not something that comes easily to the Rodowskys.

Those boys have the reddest hair I've ever seen, and each of them is covered with freckles. Shea is the oldest; he's nine. He plays Little League baseball and takes piano lessons. (What a well-rounded child!) Jackie, who's seven, is the middle child. As I said, we call him the Walking Disaster— he's *always* getting into some kind of trouble. But he has this contagious grin. When he smiles, you just can't help smiling back. Archie, the youngest Rodowsky, is just four. He's adorable, especially when he shows off the stuff he's practising for his gymnastics classes. Which is what he was doing when Dawn walked in the door that day.

"Watch me, Dawn!" he cried, as he bent over and began a somersault. "My teacher says I do these best of anyone in my class!"

Just as Archie began to roll over, Jackie ran into the room with a plate of crackers, tripped over his brother, and went flying. The crackers went flying, too. "Oh, no!" Jackie yelled. "I was going to eat those while I watched my TV show." Archie had finished his somersault and was waiting to see what happened next. He didn't even seem to realize that Jackie had tripped over him.

Jackie looked shamefacedly at Dawn, who was standing with her hands on her hips. "I didn't see Archie there," he explained. "It's not my fault, is it?"

It's *never* Jackie's fault!

"Of course not," said Dawn. "But let's clean up these crackers before they get ground into the carpet."

"Bo will help," said Shea, who had come into the room. "He's really good at cleaning up stuff like that. Here, Bo!" he called.

Bo, who happens to be a dog, came scampering into the room and headed straight for the crackers. Within seconds they had all disappeared. "See?" asked Shea proudly.

"Great," said Dawn. "Now, what's up for today? Do you have homework?" Mrs Rodowsky had run out so fast that Dawn had no idea what the boys were supposed to do.

"Not me!" said Jackie.

"I do," said Shea glumly. Then he brightened. "Hey!" he said. "Maybe you could help me. I'm supposed to find out some stuff about the history of Stoneybrook. You know, for Heritage Day. I'm supposed to learn about the families that founded the town. My teacher said I should go to the town hall and look through the records they keep there."

"Sounds fine to me," said Dawn. "I've never been there before, but I'm sure someone will be able to help us. It might be fun. What do you two think?" she asked Jackie and Archie.

"Yea!" said Jackie. "Can we take Bo?"

Dawn just looked at him.

"I suppose not," he said. "Oh, well. Poor Bo has to stay at home again." He bent to give the dog a hug. "Let's go!" he said.

Dawn helped the boys into their jackets (Jackie tore the sleeve of his because he was trying to show off how it looked when he put it on backwards) and then they headed for the town hall.

The Stoneybrook town hall is near the library. It's a big old building made of grey stone, and I've always thought it looks a bit like a prison. Dawn thought so, too, as she climbed the stairs with the boys. She pushed open the heavy door and was greeted by a musty smell and a quiet, hushed feeling. Suddenly she realized the town hall might not have been the best place to bring the Rodowsky boys. She grabbed Archie's hand and motioned to Jackie to come closer. "I want you boys to behave," she whispered. "No loud talking, no running, no touching anything that looks breakable. Understood?"

Jackie and Archie nodded solemnly. "Now, Jackie," said Dawn, sitting him down at a table. "I want you to sit here with Archie while I take Shea to the information desk. He has to find out where to do his research. Sit right here and don't move a muscle," she said. "I'll be back in a second."

She looked over her shoulder at the two of them as she walked Shea to the desk. They sat quietly, hands folded in their laps, looking like innocent little boys. Dawn smiled to herself. She *knew* they could be good if they tried.

With the help of the woman at the desk, Shea was soon settled down next to a pile of big record books. "Looks like you can find just about anything here," she said to him. And then something occurred to her. "I wonder," she said out loud. She reached for the "B" volume, planning to look up Baker and see what she could find out about my mother and grandmother. But before she could open it, she heard a loud crash from the next room—and remembered Jackie and Archie.

"Oh, no," she cried. She ran back to where she'd left them, but they were nowhere in sight. So she ran towards the room that the crash had come from. There was Jackie, standing in front of a filing cabinet, looking sheepish. The woman from the information booth was on her knees beside him, trying to scoop up an armful of folders without letting them get out of order. One of the drawers from the cabinet lay on its side on the floor.

"I'm so sorry," Dawn said to the woman.

"It's all right," she replied. "It's not the first time it's happened. These old drawers just don't stop where they should."

"I didn't *mean* to," said Jackie. "I was just checking to see whether—"

"Never mind," said Dawn, a little impatiently. "Where's Archie?"

86

"Um," said Jackie. "He said he wanted to play hide-and-seek. So I told him to hide."

"You *what*?" asked Dawn. "Where is he?"

"I don't know," said Jackie, with a shrug. "He's hiding."

Dawn rolled her eyes.

It was a long afternoon at the town hall. While Shea did his research, Dawn was kept busy with Archie and Jackie. She found Archie behind some curtains, only to have to run across the room to keep Jackie from using the photocopier to make a picture of his face. Then Archie escaped and hid again, this time in the men's toilets. Dawn had to ask one of the assistants to fetch him. Next, Jackie slid down the big banister that ran down the centre of the main stairs, almost knocking over the mayor, who was walking up to her office. And Archie escaped again while Dawn was apologizing for Jackie, and that time Dawn found him, after a *long* search, in the caretakers cupboard.

Dawn was exhausted by the time she got home that night, but she wasn't too tired to come marching into my room to tell me what she'd been thinking about all day.

"You know," she said, "I started to look for information on your mother at the town hall today."

"You did?" I asked. "Do you think there's anything there?"

87

"Whether there is or not isn't the point," she said. "I realized today that you shouldn't *have* to be looking through public records to find out what you want to know. You should be able to ask your father about it. I think it's time for you to do that."

"No," I said stubbornly. "Not my dad."

"Well," she replied. "I think you should talk to *some* adult about it."

"I couldn't," I said. "I wouldn't know what to *say*. Now, if Mimi were alive—"

"But she's not," said Dawn bluntly. "And you need information, and support. Why don't you at least talk to Kristy, or Claud? Maybe their parents told them something about this—or maybe they remember things from long ago."

Dawn was pretty convincing. It wasn't easy to get on the phone and tell Kristy what I'd discovered. She was totally shocked, and so was Claud when I called her. But neither of them could help me at all. This was the first they'd heard about my strange past.

11th CHAPTER

"Paint?"

"Check."

"Cardboard?"

"Check."

"Music?"

I held up the cassette recorder. "Check. We're ready." Dawn and I were waiting for the rest of the BSC to arrive. We had chosen Saturday as the day to create our cardboard cut-outs for Heritage Day. Dad and Sharon were running errands, as they usually do on Saturday mornings, so we had the place to ourselves.

Logan was the first to arrive, and Jessi and Mal came soon after. When Claudia arrived, she gave me a significant look and a big hug. "I'm okay," I said. "Really." I had decided to forget about my problems—at least for this one day. Telling Claud and Kristy the night before had helped me feel better, even though nothing was solved. But I wasn't ready to tell everyone else; not just yet, anyway. I'd apologized to Logan for acting so strangely, but I hadn't explained anything to him.

Kristy came in right behind Claud. She gave me a significant look, too, but instead of a hug she gave me a little punch on the arm. That's Kristy's version of a hug. It means, "I'm here for you" or something to that effect.

Stacey turned up last, and finally we were ready to start. Dawn put the latest Gary Rockman tape in the cassette player, Claud and Mal started sketching the figures onto the cardboard, and the rest of us mixed paints and spread newspapers all over the floor in the study. I'd promised Dad and Sharon we'd clean up any mess we made.

"Okay," said Claud. "Who's ready to start on Old Hickory, here?" She held up the sketch she'd done.

"Claudia, that's great!" said Dawn. "I love his outfit." Old Hickory was wearing breeches and an old-fashioned waistcoat. Dawn turned to me. "How about if you, me, and Logan work on this one?" she said. "Then Jessi and Stacey and Kristy can start on the next one."

"Sounds good," said Logan. He grabbed a brush and a jar of paint.

"Wait," I said. "Don't we have to cut him out, first?"

"Oh, right," said Logan. He put down the paint and started to walk towards the kitchen. "I'll get the scissors," he said.

"Logan!" I yelled, calling him back. "I've already got the scissors, right here."

Logan turned round quickly—and tripped over the jar of paint he'd just put down. A thick, yellow puddle spread over the newspapers.

"Quick!" I said. "Mop that up before it hits the carpet!" I tossed him a roll of paper towels.

"Don't worry," said Claud. "It's water-based. It shouldn't make any *permanent* stains."

"What about my new trainers?" asked Logan, looking down at his feet. Both trainers were smeared with yellow.

"Take 'em off," I said. "But first, catch that puddle."

Once Logan had cleaned up the paint and taken off his shoes, we were ready to start. By that time, the other team of painters were starting on a double figure: George and Martha Washington.

Dawn cut out our figure, carefully working around the hard parts. She had just finished when the tape stopped. "I'll get it," said Dawn. She jumped up, ran to the cassette player—and knocked over the jar of red paint I'd been stirring.

"Oh, no!" I cried. I grabbed the paper towels that were still sitting by Logan, and started to wipe up the mess. Some of it dripped on to my shorts, but I cleaned most of it up by the time Dawn started another tape. She turned up the volume even higher than before, and danced back to us.

"Okay, let's get to work!" she shouted, over the music.

For the next half hour, we painted steadily without any major incidents. The music was loud, and the beat kept us going.

"I *love* this portrait of Sophie!" yelled Jessi. "You guys did a great job with it."

Claud and Mal grinned. "She does look good, doesn't she?" said Mal. "Just like the original portrait." Mal had a dab of green paint on her nose, and Claud pointed it out. Mal rubbed it, but only smeared it onto her cheeks. She shrugged. "It'll come off later," she said, smiling.

Logan reached for the jar of blue paint that I'd been using, and gave it a vigorous stir. So vigorous that it splashed all over my legs. "Hey!" I said. I picked up my brush and flicked at him. It made red spots across his shirt.

That's when the paint fight began.

Soon all eight of us were covered with streaks and spots and drips. Claud had yellow paint in her eyebrows. Stacey had a red streak in her hair. Jessi had pink toes. What a mess.

Logan got the worst of it: his shirt was nearly covered with paint. "This is ridiculous," he said. "Every time I move, I get more paint on me." He unbuttoned his shirt and pulled it off.

"Woo!" said Kristy.

Logan blushed.

So did I. I've seen Logan with his shirt off before, since we've been swimming together. But somehow it was different when he was sitting right there in my study. "I'll get you one of my dad's shirts as soon as I finish painting this," I said. "I'm sure he wouldn't mind if you borrowed one." I couldn't even look at Logan as I said that; I was feeling *very* shy with him all of a sudden.

"You know what?" said Mal. "I'm starving. I brought over stuff to make cookies with. Okay if I make them now?"

"Of course," said Dawn. "Go for it."

Mal headed for the kitchen, changing the tape as she passed the cassette player. She turned it up even louder so that she'd be able to hear it while she was baking.

I looked around the room. "Boy, I hope Sharon and Dad don't come home too soon," I said to Dawn. "This place is a mess." Bits and pieces of cardboard were scattered over the table and the carpet. Paint was splattered everywhere. And my friends and I looked as if we'd been in a paint-factory accident.

Mal walked back into the room, holding

two eggs. "Hey, Mary Anne," she said. "How do you turn on your oven?"

I got up to help her, and just then Tigger dashed out from behind the sofa. Mal sidestepped to avoid him, and dropped the eggs. "Uh-oh," she said. "I'll go and get some paper towels." She ran back to the kitchen, and I started to follow her.

The doorbell rang. "I'll get it!" I yelled. I turned round and slipped in the broken eggs, but caught myself before I fell. Mal ran up behind me, paper towels in her hand, and started dabbing at my shoes. "It's okay," I said to her. "Just try to clean up the stuff on the floor."

I opened the front door, wondering who our visitor could be.

"Hello," said the woman on the front porch. "Is this the Spier-Schafer residence?" She was dressed in a navy-blue suit, stockings, and high-heels. She had a little string of pearls around her neck. And she was carrying a clipboard.

I stood there with my mouth hanging open. Who *was* this lady? "Uh, yes. Yes, it is," I replied. "Can I help you?"

"I just have a few questions to ask," she said. She peered over my shoulder, as if to get a better view of the pandemonium inside.

All at once, with a horrible, sinking feeling, I knew who she was and what she wanted. She was a social worker, and she was checking up on my father and me. She had come at the worst possible time.

"Um, my father isn't at home," I said. "I mean, he knows I have friends over, and he'd never let things get out of hand like this if he *were* here, but he's not at home right now. He'll be here any minute, I'm sure. He never leaves me alone for very long." I was babbling, and I knew it.

The woman looked at me curiously. "This will only take a few minutes," she said.

"Fine, fine," I said, edging out of the door. I was hoping that if I kept her outside on the porch, she wouldn't see what was going on.

"Most of the egg is cleaned up now," yelled Mal over the loud music that was blasting through the hall and out the door. "You two can come in, if you want. I don't think you'll slip."

"That's okay, Mal," I yelled back. I turned to the woman. "Just a little accident," I said. "She was going to bake some cookies—some *nutritious* cookies, and—"

"What's up, Mary Anne?" asked Logan from behind me. The woman gaped at him. He still wasn't wearing a shirt, he was barefoot, and his hair, which was full of yellow paint, was standing straight up.

"Logan," I hissed. "Everything's fine. Go on inside." I practically shoved him inside and slammed the door behind him. Now I was alone on the porch with the social worker. "It's not usually like this," I said, talking quickly. "It's just that all my friends—who are very responsible—are over to work on a project. It's for Heritage Day, the one that the Historical Society is putting on. So this is *educational*."

Now the social worker looked incredibly confused. "Perhaps I could come back another time," she said. "It seems as if you're busy right now. I'll call for an appointment with your father."

By then I was sure we were in trouble, but I tried to hide my panic. "That'll be fine," I said. "He'll be glad to talk to you. He has nothing to hide."

With another funny look, the woman said goodbye, and walked off carrying her clipboard. I sat down on the porch. I started to cry as soon as she was out of sight.

Logan slipped outside and sat next to me. He was wearing one of my father's shirts. Dawn must have got it for him. "What's the matter?" he asked.

"Oh, Logan," I sobbed. He put his arm around my shoulders and listened while the whole story came pouring out. "And now she's going to file a report with the authorities," I finished, still sobbing, "and I'm going to be sent off to Maynard, Iowa!"

"What's this about Iowa?" asked Stacey, who had joined us on the porch.

I didn't have the energy to tell the whole story again, so Logan repeated it for everyone. By then we were all clustered on the porch, and my friends were looking stunned.

"Mary Anne," said Jessi. "Don't you think you should talk to your father?"

"That's what I thought," said Dawn. "She just *has* to confront him about it. He's got some explaining to do."

"I can't!" I wailed. "I can't do it. What if he tells me something I don't want to know?" He'd given me up. Maybe he'd never really wanted me—even though he did fight to get me back. Maybe if I started causing trouble he'd give up on me and send me away.

"At least think about it," said Logan. He gave me a squeeze. "I hate to see you so unhappy. Now, how about if we go inside and clear up?"

12th CHAPTER

Charlotte gripped my hand tightly as we walked towards the picnic tables, which were surrounded by people. "I'm glad you came with me, Mary Anne," she whispered, looking up at me. "Look how many people are here."

"I know," I replied. "I feel a little shy, don't you?" I was sure she did, and I knew it would help if I admitted that I did, too.

We were at the parent-child picnic, which was being held on the grounds of the Historical Society. It was a beautiful day, with puffy white clouds sailing through a blue sky. I was planning to concentrate on making sure Charlotte had a good time; that way, I thought, I could forget about my own troubles for a while. "Look at the stream, Charlotte. Isn't it pretty?" I pointed to a tumbling brook edged by weeping

98

willow trees. "Maybe we can go for a paddle later."

By then we'd reached the picnic tables, which were spread with red-and-white-checked tablecloths and loaded with huge bowls and platters of food. "Wow!" I said. "There's enough food here to feed an army."

"I'm not really hungry," said Charlotte in a small voice. She was looking around at all the kids and adults who were gathered near us. Every child seemed to be with a parent; a mother, a father, or both. I realized that Charlotte was feeling strange because her own parents weren't there.

"Let's see if we can find someone we know," I said to her. "Look, there's Becca Ramsey." Becca, Jessi's eight-year-old sister, is one of Charlotte's best friends. She and her mother were inspecting the potato salad. "Hi, Becca," I said. "Hi, Mrs Ramsey."

"Well, hello, Mary Anne," said Mrs Ramsey. "How nice to see you here."

She and I talked for a minute, and then I looked round for Charlotte. She'd apparently got over her shyness; she and Becca were loading their plates with piles of food. "Hey!" I called to her. "Don't take more than you can eat, okay?"

"But we want to try everything," said Charlotte. "See, Becca is getting a spoonful from every other bowl, and I'm getting the ones in between. That way we won't miss anything."

"Good planning, girls," said Mrs Ramsey, laughing.

I loaded up a plate of my own. By the time I'd finished, Charlotte had found two more friends, and they'd all taken their plates of food down to the stream. The other girls, Corrie Addison and Haley Braddock, were at the picnic with their mothers. Soon a large group of us was sitting by the stream. I felt a little uncomfortable, since I was the only person who wasn't either a little girl or a mother, so I just concentrated on my three-bean salad.

Everyone was talking about Heritage Day. Charlotte explained her family tree project, and Corrie told us about her oral history project. She was interviewing elderly people at Stoneybrook Manor, and putting together a book of their reminiscences about the "good old days" in Stoneybrook. "This one man remembers when Stoneybrook was just a little tiny town, with a general store and a post office and not much else," she said. "Can you imagine?"

The talk went on, but my attention drifted. I looked around at the other clusters of people. There were kids with fathers, and kids with grandparents. There were even three girls with their aunt; the Craine girls, who go everywhere with their beloved Aunt

Bud. But most of the kids had come with their mothers. I'd never gone *anywhere* with my mother. We'd never gone to a picnic, or a family reunion, or even on a walk around town. I just couldn't seem to escape the fact that I didn't have a mother; that I was different. I'd thought being at the picnic with Charlotte would be a distraction, but instead I ended up dwelling on my problems again.

After we'd eaten, there were three-legged races and watermelon-seed-spitting contests and other old-fashioned games. The Historical Society had planned the picnic well. Everyone had a great time, including Charlotte, who didn't seem to miss her parents too much once she found some friends. But somehow I couldn't shake off the feeling of sadness that had come over me.

I brought Charlotte home that afternoon, and she ran to tell her mother about the picnic. Dr Johanssen thanked me for taking Charlotte and tried to pay me for my sitting time, but I wouldn't take the money. "I was glad to take her," I said. I knew how bad Charlotte's parents must have felt about not being able to go.

I walked home slowly, thinking hard. I was getting tired of feeling sad and confused about my past. Maybe it was finally time for me to confront my father and learn the truth—even if it was painful. I decided I felt so bad already that nothing I found out could make me feel much worse.

When I got home, I walked through the house looking for my dad, but he didn't seem to be around. In fact, the house was empty. Sharon and Dawn were out at the arcade, I knew that. I headed out of the back door, feeling depressed and wishing for my dad. This would be the perfect time to talk to him, when we could be alone. I sat down for a minute on the back steps, holding Tigger. "Oh, Tigger," I said, stroking him. "I know *you* understand. You probably don't remember your mother, either." Tigger looked at me and purred.

Then I heard a clicking noise, and I glanced up to see my dad standing by the hedge that runs along our property. He was holding a pair of clippers in his hand. "Dad!" I said, surprised. "I didn't think you were home." My heart started to pound. Now that he was here, I knew I had to take the plunge.

He smiled at me, put down the shears, and sat beside me. "How was the picnic?" he asked.

"Oh, fine," I said. I was thinking fast. How could I start this discussion? "Dad, there's something I want to ask you," I said.

"What is it?"

"Um," I said, "would you—would you like some lemonade? You must be thirsty."

"That would be great," he said. He leaned back. "I *have* been working for a while."

I went inside for the lemonade. I was annoyed at myself for stalling, but glad to have another minute to think things out. I poured two glasses and brought them outside.

"Thanks," said Dad. He took a big gulp. "Ah, this tastes great." Then he looked me in the eye. "Now, what did you want to ask me? I know it wasn't about lemonade. You look too serious for that."

My father is pretty sensitive sometimes. "You're right," I said. "It *was* something else. It was about—well, it was about my mother. You know, I was at the picnic, and most of the kids there were with their mums. It made me feel sad."

"Oh, darling," he said. He reached out and squeezed my shoulder. "That must have been hard."

"It was," I said. "But it wasn't the picnic that made me upset." I took a deep breath and went on. "It was something I found out. About my past. About my grandparents."

My dad looked up, surprised. "Your grandparents?" he asked. "What about them?"

"I found out that I lived with them for a while, and that they wanted me to stay with them forever. I read some letters," I rushed

103

on. "I know I shouldn't have been snooping, but I was so curious. And I also overheard that phone call you had with my grandmother." There. It was all out.

My father looked *very* surprised. "Why, Mary Anne," he said. "It's not like you to—"

"I know it's not, and I'm sorry," I said. "But you know what? I think you owe *me* an apology, too."

My father raised his eyebrows. "An apology?" he asked.

"Yes," I said. "Why did you let me think I didn't have any relatives? Why didn't you ever tell me about the time I spent in Iowa? And why did you send me there in the first place?" Suddenly I was angry. "And also, what are you going to do when the social worker tells my grandmother you're an unfit parent? She wants custody again anyway, and now she'll have no problem getting it."

"Social worker?" my dad asked. "Custody? Oh, honey, nothing like that is going to happen. That's in the past. Where did you get the idea a social worker was involved?"

I told him about the woman who had knocked on the door, and about everything she'd seen and heard: Logan with his shirt off, the music blasting, the broken eggs.

My dad's frown became a smile. "Oh, Mary Anne," he said. "You've got all upset

104

about nothing. That woman was a census taker. She just wanted to know how many people live in our house, that's all."

I heaved a huge sigh of relief. Maybe I wasn't going to be shipped off to Maynard, Iowa, after all. "But what about that phone call from my grandmother?" I asked. "She said she wants me back."

"For a visit, honey, for a visit. She just wants to see you before it's too late." My father took my hand. "Look, here's the whole story. When your mother died, I was devastated. I knew I wasn't going to be able to look after you the way I should. Not at first, anyway. So I asked Verna and Bill to look after you for a while. They loved having you, and they even tried to convince me that you should stay with them forever. But once I got back on my feet, I wanted you with me. After all, I am your father. I loved you then, I love you now, and I'll always love you." He had tears in his eyes. "There was a custody fight," he said, "but it was resolved without much fuss or bitterness. Verna and Bill realized that you belonged with me. But after that, we didn't have much to do with each other. They thought that seeing you would be too painful for them, and I agreed. That's all there is to it."

"Too painful?" I said. "Why?" I could guess, but I wanted to hear him say it.

"Because you look and behave so much

like your mother," he said, after a moment. "It used to be painful for me, too—but now it's a comfort." He reached out to hug me.

I hugged him back—hard—and there were tears in my eyes now, too. "I love you, Daddy," I said. "I'm glad you fought to get me back."

"Me, too," he said into my shoulder. "Me, too."

I went to bed that night totally exhausted, but calmer than I'd felt in days. At last I knew the truth. But I was starting to think about something else: Now I knew that I had a grandmother, and she wanted to see me. What was I going to do about that?

13th CHAPTER

Saturday

Boy, families are complicated these days. Hardly anyone has just a straightforward, normal family. Instead, they have stepfathers and stepmothers and half-sisters and stuff. It's hard to keep track of. But in some ways, it's nice. I've got all these extra people in my life, and I like that.

Kristy was thinking a lot about families that day. It was the day of the parent-child picnic—the day I ended up having that great talk with my dad. Kristy was at home, sitting for David Michael, Emily Michelle, Karen, and Andrew.

Kristy's friend Shannon Kilbourne, who's an associate member of our club, was visiting that afternoon. She'd been telling Kristy and the kids about the family reunion she'd just gone to.

"It was great," she said. "Everybody wore these T-shirts that said 'Kilbourne Family Reunion', and name tags that said who we were. Like, mine said, 'Shannon, daughter of Ted and Kathy'. I met all these cousins I didn't even know I had, and we played volleyball and horseshoes and stuff."

"That sounds cool," said Kristy. "Did you meet any really old people who knew about the history of the Kilbournes?" Kristy had been thinking a lot about history because of the Heritage Day activities.

"Yeah, that was great," said Shannon. "In the afternoon, after we'd had the picnic, all the old people got together and talked about things they'd done long ago. My uncle video taped it and he's going to make everyone a copy."

"Let's play family reunion," said Karen. "I'll be the great-great-grandmother!" She picked up a stick and started to hobble around, using it as a walking stick.

Kristy thought for a minute. "Boy, if my family had a reunion, it would be pretty complicated. I mean, I have these cousins, Ashley and Berk. What would their relationship be to Karen and Andrew? I suppose they'd be stepcousins."

"Yeah, and if your cousins had kids, they'd be step-cousins once removed!" said Shannon. "Or something like that."

"What if they had *step*kids?" asked Kristy. She was beginning to feel a little dizzy. "They'd be step-step-cousins."

"Tep! Tep!" said Emily Michelle, grinning.

"That's right, Emily," said Kristy. "You got adopted into a big family."

"One of the things they had at the family reunion was this huge chart," said Shannon. "It listed all the members of the family and showed how we're related. That helped a lot."

"We could make one of those," said Karen. She threw down her "cane" and ran to get paper and Magic Markers. Then she sprawled on the floor and started to write. "Karen Brewer," she said out loud as she wrote her name.

"That's a good start," said Kristy. "Now, put your parents' names over yours, with a line connecting them to you."

Karen added those names, and then looked at the chart, confused. "Where do I put my stepmother?" she asked.

"Draw a line next to your dad's name, and put my mother's name there," said Kristy. "Then you can draw a line down from them and put in me and Charlie and Sam and David Michael and Emily Michelle."

Karen was concentrating so hard her tongue was sticking out as she wrote the names in their proper places. "What about Nannie?" she asked.

"Nannie goes over my mum's name," said Kristy. "And then you have to put in my aunts' names over there," she pointed. "Aunt Colleen and Aunt Theo."

"Where do *I* go?" asked Andrew. He'd put down the toy he'd been playing with, and was looking over Karen's shoulder.

"Right next to me," said Karen. "Then I have to put in all of *our* aunts and uncles and cousins."

"Cousins!" Kristy said. "That's right. You have to put in all of my cousins, too. Ashley and Berk and Grace and Peter go under Aunt Colleen's name, and Luke and Emma and Beth go under Aunt Theo's. And I don't even know where my *dad's* brothers and sisters and *their* kids would go."

Shannon shook her head. "Boy, your family *is* complicated," she said. "If you ever had a family reunion, you'd have to hire a baseball stadium or something."

"That would be cool," said David

110

Michael. "Maybe our family could make a team and play againsts the Mets."

Shannon and Kristy laughed. "I *like* my big family, though," said Kristy, after she'd thought for a moment. "I'm connected to so many people in different ways. I love being a stepsister to Karen and Andrew, and I love being a granddaughter to Nannie. It's like all these people help you know who *you* are in the world."

"I know what you mean," said Shannon. "I love to hear my aunts talk about the day I was born, and what I was like as a baby."

This made Kristy think. Relatives weren't the only ones who could remember things that happened in the past. Friends could, too. And her mum had been friends with *my* mum and dad, back before I was born. Kristy decided then and there that as soon as her mum came home that day, she'd ask her more about what had happened when my mother died.

When Karen's chart was finished, it looked like a road map. There were lines going in all directions, and names scrawled everywhere. Kristy helped her hang it up, and then joined in a game of "family reunion" for the rest of the afternoon.

When her mum got home, Kristy cornered her in the kitchen. "I want to ask you something," she said.

"Why don't you help me put the

shopping away, and then we can talk," said her mum.

Kristy thought while she stacked cans of tuna-fish and tomato sauce. She didn't want to put her mum on the spot, but she was very curious.

"Come and sit down," her mother said, when the grocery bags were empty. She patted the seat beside her at the kitchen table. "Now, what did you want to talk about?"

"About Mary Anne," said Kristy. "I mean, about when Mary Anne was young. What happened when her mother died?"

"Oh," said Kristy's mum. She shook her head. "Oh, it was so sad. We all knew that Alma was ill, but none of us expected her to go so quickly. We weren't that close—your father and I had only just moved into the neighbourhood—but she was a lovely person. I remember how welcoming she was when we moved in. She brought us an almond cake, and offered to help me unpack."

"But what about afterwards?" asked Kristy. "What happened then?"

"Well, Mr Spier was just torn apart," said Kristy's mum. "He walked around looking lost. And when Mary Anne would cry, he looked confused. It was as if he had no idea how to deal with his baby girl."

"Is that why he sent her away?" asked Kristy.

112

Her mum looked at her, surprised. "Why, yes, I suppose it was," she said. "You know, I'd forgotten about that. It was so long ago. But Mary Anne did go off to live with her grandparents—in Idaho, I think it was."

"Iowa," said Kristy.

"Somewhere far away," her mother agreed. "But when she was gone, Richard looked lonelier and sadder than ever. I think he missed her very much."

"So she came back?" asked Kristy.

"As soon as he felt ready, he sent for her," said her mum. "And now that I think of it, I wonder how I ever could have forgotten that time. I remember it as if it were yesterday. One day, soon after she'd come back, I saw Richard pushing Mary Anne in her buggy. 'Look at my little girl,' he said to me. 'Isn't she beautiful?' Then I saw him smile for the first time in almost two years, and it nearly made me cry." Kristy told me later that her mother seemed close to crying that afternoon in the kitchen, just thinking about that time.

"So he always *wanted* her?" asked Kristy.

"Why, of course he did," said her mum. "She was his little girl."

"Why didn't you ever tell me this before?" asked Kristy. "Why didn't you tell Mary Anne?"

"I suppose I'd just forgotten about it," said her mum. "It was such a sad time for

113

that family. I wasn't trying to hide anything from you. Anyway, everything turned out just fine. Richard has been a wonderful father, and Mary Anne has turned out to be a happy, well-adjusted girl."

"Not so happy lately," said Kristy. She told her mother what I'd discovered, and about my fears that my father would give me up again.

"Oh, poor Mary Anne," said Kristy's mum. "I hope she's talked to her father by now, so she knows she has nothing to worry about."

That night, Kristy phoned to tell me about her talk with her mum. And I told her about the talk I'd had with my dad.

"So I suppose I got worried about nothing," I said.

"It sounds like it," said Kristy. "My mother was just a neighbour, but even she knew how much your dad loved you."

"I'm going to talk to your mum one day soon," I said. "I want to hear all about my mother. I want her to tell me everything she can remember. And you know what? I'm going to bring her an almond cake. I think my mother's recipe is still around."

14th CHAPTER

"Whoa! Watch it!" Logan stepped forward quickly to catch Old Hickory, who was about to fall on his face.

Well, not the *real* Old Hickory. It was the cardboard figure we'd made, and we were busy setting up our stall. It was Heritage Day, and the grounds of the elementary school were already full of people.

I helped Claudia set up George and Martha Washington, then stood back to take a look. "They look terrific!" I said. "Here, Kristy, take the camera. I want to see how I look with these two." I stood between the cut-out figures, put my fingers over George's head to give him rabbit ears, and made a silly face. Kristy giggled and snapped my picture with the instant camera. I let go of Martha's arm and stood next to Kristy. We watched as the picture developed, and started giggling as soon as we saw it.

"Awesome!" said Kristy. "It really looks like you're a good friend of George and Martha." The rest of the BSC gathered around to look.

"That's great!" said Jessi. "Let's stick it up on our stall so people can see how good they'll look."

"No!" I said, suddenly shy. "I don't want my picture displayed for everyone to see. Take another one. Dawn, you do it." I stuck the photo in my back pocket. Later I'd put it up on my noticeboard.

Dawn stood next to Old Hickory and put her arms around him. She gazed at him lovingly. "You're a hunk, Old Hick," she said, giggling. Stacey snapped the photo.

"That's great!" she exclaimed as soon as she saw how it had come out. "Look, you lot. Here's Dawn with her new boyfriend." We passed the picture around.

"Stacey, this was a good idea," said Kristy. I knew it took a lot for her to admit that, since Kristy is usually our "ideas" person. But she was right. I could tell that our booth was going to be a hit.

We pinned Dawn's picture on our booth, next to the sign Claudia had made. The sign said "POSE WITH STONNEY-BROOK'S SELEBRITYS." As usual,

116

Claud's spelling was a little off, but the sign was beautiful.

The booth next to ours was run by some third-graders; they were selling maps of "Olde Stoneybrook". On the other side was a booth set up by some teachers. They were selling refreshments: an old-fashioned drink called "switchel", which was made with lemonade and ginger ale, and chocolate-chip cookies, which were delicious, even if they weren't historically accurate.

As soon as we'd set up our stall, customers started to arrive. We had decided to take turns running the stall, and Dawn, Kristy, and I were on the first shift. Dawn was taking the pictures, I was helping people pose, and Kristy was collecting the money. We were pretty busy. Old Hickory turned out to be the most popular cut-out: Everybody seemed to want their picture taken with him.

After a while, Jessi, Mal, and Claud relieved us. Kristy went off to find David Michael, Karen, and Andrew. Dawn and I started to walk around the fair, looking at the stalls.

"Extra! Extra! Read all about it!" yelled Jordan Pike. He was walking towards us, holding up a copy of the *Olde Stoneybrook News* that his class had published. He was dressed like a newsboy from long ago, in knickerbockers, a tank-top, and a cap. But instead of old-fashioned shoes, he was wearing his green trainers with fluorescent-orange laces. "Extra!" he shouted again. "Doc Swanson buys town's first horseless carriage! Neighbours say it'll never take the place of the horse!"

We stopped him and bought a copy of the paper. "This is great," said Dawn. "The kids really worked hard on it. Look at this picture they found of the town after that big blizzard!" She showed me the paper.

Next we stopped at a little stage that had been set up near the baseball diamond. Claire Pike's class was singing the songs they'd learned. They sounded a little out of tune, and a little unsure of the words, but I could tell they were having fun. I caught Claire's eye and gave her a wink. She was dressed in a pilgrim outfit like all the others (no feather boa this time), and she looked great.

After the little kids had finished, the second-graders performed their sketch. Margo said her lines perfectly; the only problem was that she giggled every time she looked at the boy who was playing her husband. The audience didn't seem to mind, though. They gave the actors a big hand when the sketch was over.

Next was Vanessa's class, reciting her epic poem. Dawn and I stayed for about eight verses, and then we gave each other a look. The poem was great, but it was time to move on.

Next to the stage was a big display of the family trees that various kids had made. I saw Charlotte standing in front of her project. Both of her parents were with her, and Charlotte was beaming as she showed off her work to the people clustered around. "Hi, Charlotte," I said. "Wow, you did a great job." She had, too. She'd made a montage of the pictures she'd found, and next to it was a beautifully drawn tree, with names on each branch. She'd also written a description of why and how her great-grandmother had originally come to Stoneybrook. It was because the town needed a hat maker, and that's what she was!

Dawn and I walked around the rest of the fair. We saw the mural that Myriah Perkins's class had made, and the project on the town's founders that Shea Rodowsky had helped with. We stopped to listen to the tapes that Corrie Addison had made at Stoneybrook Manor. And we ate and ate: cookies and hot dogs and popcorn. Then we went back to our stall.

"How's business?" I asked. By that time the third shift had taken over: Stacey, Logan, and Shannon were watching the booth.

"It's slowed down a little," said Logan. "I think nearly every person here has already had their picture taken!"

"You should have seen how Mr Pike looked with Sophie," said Stacey. "They made quite a couple."

"We took in a lot of money," said Shannon, who was busy counting it. "The Historical Society will be happy to have this!" She held up a wad of notes.

At the end of the day, I helped take down the cut-outs. Dawn and I had agreed to store them in our barn, just in case they'd ever come in handy again. My dad came by to drive us—and the figures—home. Dawn and I told him about the fair as he drove.

"It was really good fun," said Dawn. "I feel as if I know a lot more about Stoneybrook now, and it wasn't boring to learn all that history. I'm going to spend some time in the library next week. Maybe I can finally find out more about Jared Mullray."

"Jared Mullray?" asked my dad.

"You know, the crazy guy whose ghost haunts our house."

My father nodded. "Oh, right," he said. "*That* Jared Mullray." He pulled into the drive and helped Dawn and me carry the cut-outs into the barn. As we emerged, dusting off our hands, he turned to Dawn. "Would you mind leaving Mary Anne and me alone for a little while?" he asked her. "There's something I need to talk to her about."

120

Dawn nodded. "Of course," she said. She squeezed my hand. "I'll be in my room, reading."

Dad took my hand and led me to his study. I was dying of curiosity—and was also a little nervous. "What is it Dad?" I asked, after he'd shut the door behind us.

"Well," he said slowly. "I think the time has come to give this to you." He put his hand into his jacket pocket and pulled out an envelope.

I took it and looked it over. It was yellowed with age, and my name was written on the front.

"It's a letter," he said. "A letter for you. It's from your mother." His voice sounded a little strange, as if he were trying to hold back tears. "She wrote it just before she died, and asked me to give it to you when you turned sixteen. But I think she'd want me to give it to you now, instead. She had no way of knowing how mature you'd be at thirteen. I hope it will help to answer some of the questions you have about your past." He sounded formal, like someone making a presentation of a medal or something.

I gulped. "Dad, are you sure?" I asked. I held the letter tightly. "I mean, do you think I'm really ready to read this?" All of a sudden I felt like a little girl again. After all my curiosity, now I wasn't sure I could handle reading my mother's words.

"You're ready, sweetheart," said my dad. He stood up and gave me a big hug. "You're ready. Why don't you take that to your bedroom and read it in private?"

"Okay," I replied, a little shakily. I left the study and went to my bedroom. I closed the door behind me and sat down on my bed, with Tigger on my lap. I was still clutching the envelope. I turned it over in my hands and looked again at my name, written in script. "My mother wrote that," I said to Tigger. "This letter is from her to me." I sat for a few more minutes, just thinking. What I held in my hands was something I'd longed for for so many years. Reading this letter would be like hearing my mother speak to me. I took a few deep breaths, and then, when I felt ready, I carefully tore open the envelope and pulled out the letter. It was written on pale blue paper, and the writing covered three whole pages.

I started to read.

"Dearest Mary Anne," it began. "How I wish I could see your face as you read this letter. Is it a face I would recognize? I know one thing for sure: it's a lovely face. The baby who sits by me as I write this is the most beautiful baby I've ever seen. (Of course, I may be a little prejudiced, since I *am* her mother.)

I smiled as I read that. The letter went on. "I know that your father loves you very much, and that he'll do everything he can to bring you up well. I know, too, that it will be hard for him and that he will need help now and then. That's why I am happy to know that my mother and father, who dote on you, are ready and willing to do whatever it takes to make sure that you have a happy and secure childhood."

I thought of the people I'd seen in the old pictures. They had kind, gentle faces. They had loved me, my grandparents—and by taking care of me they had been carrying out a promise they'd made to my mother. I let go of any mean thoughts I'd had about my grandmother.

"Mary Anne," the letter went on. "I would give anything to be with you today— to be with you through all your days of growing up. I love you so much, and it hurts so badly to know that I have to leave you."

That's when I started to cry.

I read the rest of the letter, crying the whole time. My mother told me about herself and her childhood. She told me how she and my father had met and fallen in love. She wrote about her hopes and dreams for me, and the hopes and dreams she'd once had for herself. By the time I'd finished the letter, I felt exhausted. But I also felt happy. Reading that letter was an experience I will never forget.

I sat alone in my room for a long time, holding the letter. Then I put it away in a special place, and went to find my father. It was time for me to make plans for a trip to Maynard, Iowa.

15th CHAPTER

Dear Dad,

Well, here I am in Maynard, Iowa. Actually, I'm not in Maynard - I'm outside it, about four miles out of town. Grandma's house sits in the middle of a huge field of corn. She doesn't farm her land herself any more, of course. She rents it out to the farmer down the road. Anyway, it's really pretty here even if it is totally flat. And Grandma is wonderful. She wants to know everything about me - what music I like, what my hobbies are, how school is for me. Mainly she wants

125

to know what I like to eat. She has been stuffing me every day with all of my favourite things: fried chicken, blueberry pie, homemade bread. I'm going to weigh six hundred pounds by the time I get home!

Grandma has lots of pictures of Mom. We go through the scrapbooks together and she tells me stories about when Mom was a little girl. She sounds a lot like me. She was sensitive and shy and she loved animals. Sometimes Grandma gets a little choked up when she talks about Grandpa, but most of the time we just have fun looking at the pictures.

Daddy, I want to thank you again for taking me to the cemetery the day before I left. It means a lot to me to know where my mother is buried. I hope we can go there together once in a while.

I think I'd like to plant
a rosebush there.
    I miss you and Sharon
and Dawn. See you soon.
                Love,
                Mary Anne
P.S. Please hug Tigger for me.

Dear Mary Anne,
    I miss you so much! I read
the letter you wrote to your dad,
so I know you're having a good
time. But I hope you'll come
home soon!
    I played with Tigger for about
an hour last night, but I think
he still misses you. He sleeps on
your bed every night, even though
I told him he could sleep with me.
    The big news here is that our
booth made the most money of
any booth at Heritage Day! The
BSC got a really nice thank-you
letter from the Historical Society.
At our club meeting yesterday
Kristy got excited and started
to talk about all kinds of wild
schemes to raise money, but we

told her to can it. We just want to be a normal club for a while.

Are there any cute boys in Iowa? You can tell me. I promise not to tell Logan. Write soon!

Your best friend and step sister 4-ever,
Dawn

Dear Kristy,

You wouldn't believe how quiet it is here, or how many stars you can see at night. I kind of like Iowa, even though there is absolutely nothing to do here. The town of Maynard consists of one traffic light, a church, a bar, and a general store. Oh, and a feed store, where you buy stuff like pig vitamins. There's no cinema, no shops no nothing.

I have to admit that I was getting a little bored for a while, but lately things have picked up. Guess what I did yesterday. I babysat. It seems like no matter where we BSC members go, we find jobs. I sat for the family at the next farm over, and boy, are these farm kids tough. They ran me ragged. I had to chase after them all day, from the barn to the garden to the attic to the cellar. They teased the cows and tried to ride the pigs. One of the boys even climbed up on the porch roof and was about to jump off before I stopped him. (He said he'd done it before, and that he was allowed, but I had my doubts.)

My grandmother is a pretty neat lady, and I like being with her. Knowing her makes me feel more connected to my mother — does that

make sense to you?
Maybe you'll meet her
one day if she comes to
visit me and my dad.
    That's all for now. It's
time to help shell peas
for dinner! (Don't I
sound like a farm girl?)
                Yours 'til Niagara Falls,
    Mary Anne

DEAR MARY ANNE,
    HOW IS IOWA? HOW IS YOUR GRAND-
MOTHER? HAVE YOU MILKED A COW
YET? NOTHING HAS CHANGED IN
STONEYBROOK. I GOT A NEW
BASEBALL MITT YESTERDAY. I
MISS YOU A LOT. PLEASE COME
HOME SOON!   LOVE, LOGAN

Dear Dawn,
    You won't believe it!
I feel so guilty. I got a
letter from Logan yesterday,
on the very same day
that I agreed to go out
on a date with another
boy!

He's the grandson of one of my grandmother's best friends. His name is Bob, and he's really, really cute. You know what, though? I have a feeling he only asked me out because his grandmother told him to. I overheard my grandmother on the phone the other day (I _wasn't_ snooping — I just heard the conversation by accident) and it sounded like she and her friend were hatching a plot. Then, the next thing I knew, Bob had stopped by to ask me out.

I wonder what we'll do. After all, there isn't much to do here. Still, it'll be fun to be with someone my own age. As much as I love my grandmother, I do miss talking about stuff like school and TV.

Please don't ever, EVER tell Logan about this thing with Bob. I'll let you know how it went next time I write.

 Love you lots,
 Mary Anne

Dear Dawn,

 Well, Logan has nothing to worry about. Bob may be cute, but he and I have absolutely nothing in common. He took me to the Dairy Queen for our date, and he ate enough for four people while I picked at my fries. He talked the whole time, and he was incredibly boring. All he wanted to talk about was what kind of car he was going to buy when he'd saved up enough money. Then he asked me if I liked cows, and when I said I didn't totally _love_ them, he looked at me like I was mad.

I suppose that's what Maynard boys are like. Give me my Stoneybrook sweetie any day!

See you next week. Say hi to all the other BSC members for me.

Love,
Mary Anne

Dear Logan,

Thanks for your letter. No, I haven't milked a cow yet, and to tell you the truth, I don't have any _plans_ to milk a cow. I miss you too — a _lot_. But I'm having a good time here, getting to know my grandmother. She's really neat. I think you'd like her. See you soon!

Love ya,
Mary Anne

Dear Mary Anne,

This is a joint letter from the BSC. As alternate officer, I've been taking over your job as secretary. Believe me, I'll be happy when you get back. I don't know how you keep track of all of this information. Anyway, things are going well here, but I'll let the others tell you the news.

Love, Dawn

Hi, Mary Anne! We all miss you. You should see the earrings Claud is wearing today — they look like little palm trees. I sat for Jackie Rodowsky yesterday, and he broke a vase, spilled lemonade all over the rug, and fell down the stairs. So, in other words, nothing is new. See ya soon!

Luv, Stacey

Dear Mary Ane,

Their not plam trees, their cactuses. Stacy doesnt know a cactis when she sees one. Anyway, we miss you. When you get back, ill show you my latest

art project: a scupture of a cow (you
can help me with the detales, since you're
spending all your time with cows latley.)
                    Love and xxx
                        Claud

Dear Mary Anne,
    Mal and I
just wanted to
say hi. We sat
for her brothers
and sisters
yesterday, and
unfortunately it
was raining, so
we were all
cooped up inside.
Luckily, we survived.
            Love, Jessi

    Well, Jessi might have survived, but she
got to go home to her nice quiet house.
I had to stay cooped up with all my
dear siblings. Maybe I should move to
Iowa, where there aren't so many people.
What do you think?
                    Love, Mal

Dear Mary Anne,
    As your chairman, I hearby order
that you COME HOME SOON. This
club doesn't run nearly as well

135

without you. Anyway, I miss my best friend. Don't forget to bring me a souvenir!

Love, Kristy

Dear Mary Anne,

I've made plane reservations for you to come home next Tuesday. I hope that's okay with you. Sharon and Dawn and I will be waiting to meet you at the airport. I can't wait to see my girl again. Give my love to Verna.

Love, Dad

Dear Dad,

What would you think of asking Grandma to come visit us sometime soon? I know she'd love to see where we live, and meet my friends. Maybe there were times in the past when you and she didn't get along that well, but I think you'd like her company now. Please think it over. I'll see you on Tuesday — I can't wait — and we can talk then.

Love, Mary Anne

Dear Grandma,

Thanks so much for inviting me to visit you in Maynard. I loved getting to know you and learning all about your life. It was also great to find out more about my mother. Now I feel as if I know who she was, and you know what? I think I am a lot like her.

When I arrived at the airport yesterday, there was a big crowd to meet me. My father and Sharon and Dawn were there, of course, but they'd also brought all my friends with them — the ones in that club I told you about. Kristy was there, and Claudia and Stacey and Jessi and Mal. It was great. I really felt like I was coming home.

But now I also feel like I have another home, another place where I will always be welcome. And that home is with you, in Maynard. I hope I'll be able to visit again soon. And Dad and I had this great idea about how you could — but I'll let him tell you all about it. I know he's writing to you, too.

Thanks again for a fantastic visit.

Love,
Mary Anne

P.S. I miss your biscuits already!

Dear Verna,

Mary Anne had a wonderful time with you. We're glad to have her back— but I'm also glad the visit was such a positive experience for her. I'm only sorry we didn't realize earlier how much you and she would mean to each other. I'd like to ask you to join us for Christmas this year. We'd love to have you, if you think you could make the trip. And, in any case, I know that Mary Anne is eager to visit you again next summer.

Fondly, Richard